THE EXCITING ADVENTURES OF JONATHAN AND JASMINE ON ANDROS ISLAND

JACQUALYN B. HANNA

The Exciting Adventures of Jonathan and Jasmine on Andros Island

Printed in the United States of America

First Edition: November 2007

Second Edition: January 2020

ISBN : 978-1-312-75671-7

Dedication

This book is dedicated to my children Jonathan and Jasmine who inspired me to tell them original bedtime stories every night. It is also dedicated to my parents who have inspired me all my life with stories and folktales which they grew up with. I am also grateful to the students of Grade 4 at Fresh Creek Primary School, 2006/2007 who told me that my stories were good. Above all, I dedicate this book to God, my heavenly father who taught me how to walk out on faith.

Acknowledgement

Special thanks are due to my niece Alicia who edited the stories, provided photographs and motivated me to publish my books. Thanks is also extended to my sisters Daverley, Princess and Diann who assisted with the word processing and proofreading, and for that I am indeed grateful. I am also thankful to Vincent who entertained the children while I remained glued to the computer. Thanks are also due to all of my siblings who provided me with the constant love and support that I needed to become the person that I am.

A Word from the Author

This children's book features fourteen stories written by Jacqualyn B. Hanna. The stories are fictitious but every story is filled with factual information about the island of Andros and the Androsian heritage. Animals that are indigenous or common to Andros are also featured in the stories. The first story that the writer decided to record was Jonathan: the Chickcharnie, the Mermaid and the Harbor Master which express the mythical beliefs of many Androsians. Most of the stories that follow are a continuation of Jonathan's adventure.

Other stories such as Jonathan and the Sea Monster and Jonathan and the Fight for the Pirate's Treasure were inspired solely by Jonathan, the writer's son as he insisted on having original bedtime stories read to him every night.

Each story is intended to teach the reader about the history of Andros, the people, the land and the environment while providing at the same time a little folklore. The stories also contain factual information on the history, geography and culture of The Bahamas.

The stories may be used in the classroom to promote reading as the writer uses repetition of words for that very purpose. The stories may also be used in Listening and Reading Comprehension classes and for that purpose the writer has provided a list of questions to accompany each story. The questions can be modified to suit the ability levels of students from grade 4 through grade 9.The stories may also be used to increase vocabulary development and spelling skills. The student's grammar skills and writing skills can also be developed through the additional questions provided.

The writer hopes that the students through the reading of these original stories will learn to decipher information by determining what is factual and what is fictional. Students should also learn to make inferences, comparisons, and connections, draw conclusions, summarize information, find the main idea, identify details and suggest different outcomes. The writer hopes that by the end of the book, students will be inspired enough to create stories of their very own.

Table of Contents

CHAPTER 1

JONATHAN THE CHICKCHARNIE, THE MERMAID AND THE HARBOR MASTER

On an island in The Bahamas known as Andros Island, there lived a boy named Jonathan. Jonathan was an only son and loved to spend most of his time playing outside. His sister Jasmine was seven years younger than he was and not considered exciting company. He would try to catch butterflies, helicopters (dragon flies) and little birds. When he got bored, he would ask his mother to tell him stories of Chickcharnies, Mermaids and the Harbor master. The Chickcharnie was a creature that was half man and half bird and believed to live in the pine forest that surrounded his home. The Chickcharnie made his home at the top of two pine trees that came together. The creature had a funny appearance but if one laughed at the Chickcharnie then that person would have extreme bad luck. However, if one did not laugh at the creature but treated it with respect, then one would become very rich. In North Andros the elders spoke of a girl who once saw a Chickcharnie and thought that the creature looked so funny that she pointed at it and laughed. She laughed so hard that she fell to the ground. When she got up, she found that one of her legs had grown and was longer than the other. From that day she walked with a limb and exactly like the Chickcharnie. Everywhere she went, people called her the Chickcharnie girl.

A mermaid was a half woman, half fish that lived in the blue holes that were in great abundance on the island of Andros. A blue hole was a large body of water in the ground and the water was so deep that it appeared blue from above. Some of the brave children went diving and swimming in the blue holes and every now and again one of them would go missing, never to be seen or heard of again. The older people in the village would warn the children not to go swimming alone in the blue holes because the mermaids would take you away. However, the older people of Blanket Sound, a little village on Andros Island told of a man who had met a mermaid at a blue hole and held her by the hair. In return for her freedom the mermaid promised him a pot of gold but in return he must never tell anyone of her existence. The man agreed and when he returned home he met a pot of gold.

But after a while he could not keep the secret to himself and shared it with his relatives. The next time he went to the blue holes, he never returned.

The Harbor Master was a giant snake that lived in the lake not far from Jonathan's home. It was said that the snake was so huge and so long that it took hours for it to cross the road. The snake did not have any natural enemies and lived of the many ducks and fish that lived in the lake. People who went in search of crabs were careful to keep an eye open for the Harbor master. Those who went for crabs and never returned were thought to be eaten by the Harbor master. A woman on Love Hill called Dorleen once saw the Harbor master through the white road on her way for crabs. She came out of the road screaming, "It's the Harbor master!" She never went crabbing through the White road again.

Even though Jonathan's mother told him of these stories Jonathan did not believe any of them. He often laughed when his mother was through and would humor her by telling her how he would one day capture the Chickcharnie and Mermaid and slay the Harbor Master.

One day as Jonathan was walking through the pine forest he was startled by a sudden noise. He looked up and there he saw the strangest creature he had ever seen. It was perched at the top of two pines trees that touched each other. It seemed unaware of Jonathan's presence and continued to dry its feathers in the golden ray of the sun. The creature had a head that resembled a human's and a face that had human characteristics, however, its body was that of a bird. Jonathan remembered what his mother had told him about the Chickcharnie and decided to leave it alone. The Chickcharnie smiled at Jonathan as he crept quietly out of the forest. When he felt he was a safe distance away, Jonathan raced home as fast as he could to tell his mother what he had seen. His mother was frightened and asked him quickly "Did you laugh at it?"

"No mother" Jonathan replied. "I remembered what you had told me and snuck away unnoticed. "A good boy!" replied his mother.

That night Jonathan's mother heard a knock at the door. She went and answered it but did not see anyone there. She looked down on the step and there she saw a pot of gold glistening in the moonlight. She fainted.

The next day, Jonathan went swimming in the blue hole. He was enjoying his swim and came up many times to dive from the top of the cliff into the water. While he was catching a little break and sat motionless on top of the cliff, he saw something moving below the surface of the water. He waited eagerly for the thing to surface and when it did he almost swallowed the little pebble he had in his mouth.

A beautiful young girl with very long hair and a tail of a fish emerged from the water and sat on the rock across from Jonathan. The Mermaid did not see Jonathan and played with her hair and at the same time, splashed her tail in the water. Jonathan stared at her for what seemed a century, not believing his eyes but remembering every word his mother had told him. After a while the Mermaid looked across the blue hole and smiled at Jonathan. "Would you like a lock of my hair she asked him?" Jonathan was speechless and could only nod his head. The mermaid jumped into the water and in no time she was wading in front of him. "You must never tell anyone," she said, "Or you will not be granted treasures."

"Can I at least tell my mother?" Jonathan asked. "Very well, but only your mother and not another single soul." With those words the mermaid handed Jonathan a lock of her hair and dived below the surface.

Jonathan dashed home to tell his mother. At first she was very afraid, "You should not have told me" she said.

With a hug and a kiss, Jonathan comforted his mother, "Don't worry mother, the mermaid said I could tell you but no one else."

Jonathan's mother was relieved. She loved her son very much and did not want to lose him for all the treasures in the world. Later that day as Jonathan and his mother were working in the garden, they unearthed a treasure chest. The treasure chest looked as if it belonged to one of the Spanish galleons that passed through Bahamian waters in the 1500's on their way to Spain. When Jonathan and his mother opened the chest, they found it to be filled with pure gold coins, pearls and treasures of every kind. They both knew that they would be rich for the rest of their lives. They had only to remember to never speak of Jonathan's encounter with the Mermaid to anyone.

The next day, Jonathan decided to go for a walk in the forest. He was feeling happy and was hoping to get a glimpse of the Chickcharnie or the Mermaid. While he was walking, he heard a ruffling in the bushes. He stood still. He watched mesmerized as the bushes seem to part themselves. After what seemed like an eternity, he recognized what was parting the bushes. It was nothing else but the Harbor Master his mother had warned him about.

Jonathan could not believe the size of the creature as it moved slowly along. The moment it spotted Jonathan, he knew he was in trouble. The creature was hungry and Jonathan looked like a nice meal. It moved toward Jonathan but Jonathan was so afraid, he could not move. Just as the giant reptile was about to swallow Jonathan, the Chickcharnie swooped down from the top of the pine trees and carried Jonathan safely into his nest. However, the snake was determined to have a meal and it wrapped itself around the trunk of the tree causing it to bend. As the tree bent with the weight of the snake, Jonathan began to scream. His screams were so loud that the Mermaid heard it from far below the water. She came to the surface as quickly as she could and shouted to Jonathan to jump into the water. Jonathan did as the Mermaid instructed him and jumped.

The Mermaid took him below the surface and into a cave that was as dry as the land above. The cave was filled with all kinds of wonderful antiques and treasures. She handed Jonathan a sword that must have belonged to one of the Spanish conquistadors that had passed through The Bahamas, and then assisted him to return to the surface. When Jonathan returned to the surface he found that the pine trees had fallen on the big snake and he was temporarily trapped. Jonathan grasped this opportunity to use the sword and cut off the head of the large snake. After thanking the Chickcharnie and the Mermaid for their help, Jonathan rushed home to show his mother his new trophy. His mother was shocked but happy that her son had returned unharmed. Everyone, from every town and settlement came to see Jonathan's new trophy. He became known as a hero and the bravest little boy on the entire island of Andros. The American Museum of natural history came and took the snake away. Jonathan was paid very well for his trophy for it was discovered that the snake was not an ordinary snake but was related to a dragon that was believed to be extinct. So Jonathan became known as the boy who slew the dragon.

CHAPTER 2

JONATHAN AND THE SEARCH FOR
THE ARAWAK VILLAGE

One day Jonathan asked his mother to tell him a story about the strange people who lived on the West side of Andros. Jonathan had heard the elders in his village of Love Hill, talk about these brown skinned people with long straight black hair. Jonathan's mother sat down and began to tell him the story. Legend had it that the archipelago of The Bahamas was once inhabited by some quiet, peaceful people known as the Arawaks. Some people referred to them as the Lucayans. These people lived happily until the coming of the Spaniards who took them away to other countries to work as slaves. However, there was a tribe of Arawaks who escaped the Spaniards and came to live on the West Coast of Andros where the wildlife was in great abundance. This tribe of Arawaks lived by farming and hunting. They hunted the huge Manatee, also known as the Sea Cow, the Alligators, the Iguanas and the pink Flamingoes. The Arawaks lived in caves that were hidden by the dense forests. Some of the caves were actually located below the surface of some blue holes. Every time a Spanish galleon sank loaded with treasure, the Arawaks would take the treasure off the shallow banks and hide them in their cave villages. Everyone knew that if you found an Arawak village you would become the richest person who ever lived," Jonathan's mother told him. Before

Jonathan's mother could finish the story, Jonathan shouted: "Mummy, I am going to find that Arawak village!"

"It's not that easy, Jonathan's mother replied, to find the village you would have to capture the four animals that the Arawaks hunted and used to make their famous stew known as pepperpot. The five animals include the Manatee that lives in the sea, the Alligator that lives in the swamps and lakes, the iguanas that live in the thick coppice and the flamingos that live in the creeks on the west side of the island. It is believed that a Spanish priest in the 1500's had discovered the secret tribe of Arawaks but because he did not want them to suffer the tragic fate of the other Arawak tribes he engraved a map of pure gold to conceal the location of the village. The map was made into four sections. A section was given to each of the four animals that the Arawaks hunted and used to make pepperpot. These animals became guardians of the secret village but if the four sections were ever placed together one would know the location of the secret Arawak village. To find the village you must first find the four guardians because each of these animals knows where you can find a section of the golden map." "I know I can capture all of these animals and convince them to share their secret," Jonathan exclaimed.

The next day, Jonathan went to his Grandpa Roy to ask him what he had to do and what he needed to capture the animals. Grandpa Roy was very knowledgeable about the island of Andros. He had hunted and ate iguanas, flamingos and sea cows. He was also one of the best sailors on the island and once captained his own vessel called "The Adeline". Grandpa Roy told him to take with him a goggle, metal wires, a cage, a butcher's knife, a rope, a sack, some fruits and a net. He told Jonathan that he would know how to use them when the time came, however, he must never let the creature go until he has gotten the information he needed.

The next day, Jonathan started out on his journey. He first went to the settlement of Fresh Creek where the Manatee was often sighted in the Fresh Creek Harbor. Jonathan waited until he saw the Manatee pass under the bridge and then he put on his goggles and jumped from the top of the bridge onto the Manatee's back. At this point the Manatee dived under the water but Jonathan held on tightly.

Tied the rope around the mouth of the creature and rode it like a horse. After what seemed like an hour the Manatee came up for air. To Jonathan's amazement the animal spoke to Jonathan, "Why are you trying to capture me?"

"I want you to tell me how to find the Arawak's village," Jonathan replied.

"If I tell you what I know would you let me go?" asked the Manatee.

"You have my word," Jonathan told the animal. "Well, let me go and I will tell you," replied the Manatee.

"No way, you must tell me what you know and then I will let you go!" Jonathan shouted.

"Very well!" replied the Manatee and with that he dived below the surface and took Jonathan to a sunken ship.

On the deck of the ship was a small treasure chest which Jonathan attached to his rope and then the Manatee returned to the surface with Jonathan on his back.

When Jonathan opened the treasure chest, he discovered the first of the four sections of the map. The first section of the map was made of pure gold and Jonathan could make out the shape of the Andros Island. Overjoyed and excited, Jonathan thanked the

Manatee as he released him and continued on his journey. The Manatee left Fresh Creek Harbor never to be seen there again. Perhaps he migrated to the Florida everglades.

Jonathan went in search of the Alligator. He knew that alligators loved to live in the swamps and lakes and so he walked many miles until he reached a deserted settlement known as Twin Lakes. Jonathan waited on the edge of the lake until he saw two big eyes on the surface of the water. He knew it was the alligator as it approached him very quietly. The alligator was hoping to have Jonathan for lunch but as he snapped at Jonathan, Jonathan jumped up into the air and landed on the reptile's back. The reptile snapped ferociously in an effort to shake Jonathan off but Jonathan threw the net over the head of the creature and then tied his mouth shut with metal wires. After that, Jonathan dragged the creature onto the land and told him that he would only let him go if he told him where to find the Arawak's village. "I will never tell you!" growled the alligator.

"Well," said Jonathan, "If you do not tell me what you know I will have to skin you and use your hide to make me some alligator boots." When Jonathan pulled out the butcher's knife the alligator became frightened and began to give the location of the second section of the map. The alligator told Jonathan to go to the middle of the lake and he would see a big buttonwood tree growing in the Centre. He must then dig three feet at the base of the tree and he would find a small treasure chest. Jonathan did as the alligator instructed him and found the treasure chest. He opened the chest and discovered the second section of the golden map. Jonathan returned to the alligator, thanked him for his help and released him. The alligator was relieved that he had regained his freedom and swam to the deepest part of the lake. The alligator was never seen in the lake again; perhaps he migrated to the Florida Everglades. Jonathan continued on his journey. He knew he had to find the iguana with the third section of the map. Grandpa Roy had told him that Iguanas loved fruits and berries and so he set up his wire cage and placed the fruits and berries inside. Before long, the Iguana spotted his fruits and berries and headed straight for them but once inside the cage, Jonathan pulled the string and the cage door closed trapping the Iguana inside. The Iguana tried frantically to escape but he could not. Jonathan went over to the Iguana smiling with delight.

"You may help yourself to all the fruit you like Mr. Iguana all I would like to know is where I can find the Arawak's village."

"Why do you believe I know where the village is?" asked the Iguana.

"Because you were given a chest by a priest hundreds of years ago and I know you have secured it well," said Jonathan.

"If I tell you where you can find the chest, will you let me go?" asked the Iguana.

"You have my word," Jonathan reassured the Iguana. The Iguana instructed Jonathan to go to Centre of the coppice where he would see a huge Mahogany tree. Ten feet to the left of the Mahogany tree is a huge sink hole. He must use a rope and lower himself down into the hole. When he reaches the bottom, he will see a tunnel. Follow the tunnel to the very end. At the end of the tunnel he will come upon a blue hole. He must dive into the blue hole and at the bottom of the blue hole he will see a treasure chest. Jonathan did exactly as the Iguana instructed and discovered the treasure chest. He returned with the third section of the golden map. Jonathan thanked the Iguana and set him free. The Iguana was so happy to have his freedom that he raced across the coppice leaving all the fruits and berries behind. The Iguana was in a hurry to migrate to Iguana Cay.

Jonathan continued on his journey. He had three sections of the golden map and he could almost decipher the location of the Arawak village. He could tell that the inscriptions were written in Spanish and there was a drawing of Andros Island. There was also a symbol of the cross and an incomplete compass. Jonathan needed the fourth section to see the compass clearly. Jonathan decided to climb the highest tree to see if he would spot the flamingo. Most of the flamingos had left Andros Island and made their home in Inagua because the natives over hunted them and ate them. Grandpa Roy had told Jonathan on many occasions how tasty the Flamingo was and how when cooked, they did not have to use any tomato paste as the flamingos produced pink gravy.

As Jonathan sat motionlessly in the tree, he felt a branch near him move. He looked to the left and could not believe his eyes. The pinkest flamingo in the entire Bahamas had perched on the branch next to him. Jonathan carefully knotted his rope and tossed it around the beautiful bird. As the bird tried to fly away, Jonathan tightened his rope and it knotted itself around the long legs of the bird. The bird now hung upside down on Jonathan's rope. "Let me go!" exclaimed the bird "Not until you tell me where I can find the Arawak's village!" Jonathan replied. "If I tell you what I know, will you let me go?"

"Yes, I will let you go. You have my word," Jonathan replied. So the pink flamingo gave Jonathan instructions to find the fourth section of the map. Jonathan was told to follow the edge of the coast until he comes upon some very thick red and black mangroves growing together. He must then make his way through the mangroves that opens up to a river. Afterwards, he must then follow the river upstream to its source. The source of the river is a cave on top of a very high hill. When he enters the cave, he would see a huge rock with water rushing out of it. He must walk under the water fall into a cavern and there he would discover the fourth treasure chest. Jonathan did as the Flamingo instructed him, found the chest and then returned to the tree and thanked the bird for his help. After he released him, the bird flew away, perhaps to Inagua.

Jonathan now had all for sections of the golden map and he carefully put it together.

He now knew the location of the Arawak's village but suddenly he felt uneasy. "Maybe I should melt down the golden map and use the money to live richly. Maybe I should leave the Arawak village undiscovered as the Spanish priest intended," Jonathan said aloud. However, Jonathan was driven by a need to know whether the village existed and so he continued his search for the village. Jonathan followed the directions on the map which took him through the pine forest and then the thick coppice, over the scrub land and through the swamp until he arrived on the West Coast of Andros. He was beginning to feel disappointed because the directions ended in the sea. "Surely, the village cannot be in the sea," Jonathan said to himself. Jonathan began to walk into the sea and then suddenly he began to fall. It was as if he had fallen into a blue hole in the sea. Jonathan passed out and when he woke up he found himself lying on a beach surrounded by medium height, brown skinned people with long straight black hair. The men were armed with bows and arrows and they looked very tensed. Both the men and women wore very little clothing. Some wore jewelry made of seashells and animal bones but some had gold ornaments on them as well. Jonathan knew that these people must be the

Arawaks and he made signs to let them know that he did not want to hurt them.

One of the Arawak men came forward and took the golden map out of Jonathan's hand and began Priest.

Then Jonathan could not believe his luck when they took him to a fountain that they proclaimed was the Fountain of Youth. They told Jonathan that no one ever died and that everyone remained the same age. They also told Jonathan of a strange man who had come looking for the Fountain of Youth but they sent him to a smaller island to the West of Andros. The village was a vibrant, happy village with the old, middle age and many children. Jonathan lived with the Arawaks for many moons, enjoying their simple way of life but after a while he got homesick and thought of his mother who must be worried sick He told his new friends that he had to return to Love Hill but he promised that he would never tell a single soul of how to find the Arawak's village or even let them know that the legend of the Arawak village was true. Jonathan surrendered the golden map to the Arawaks and in return they gave Jonathan a treasure chest of unspeakable riches. Jonathan went to sleep in preparation for his journey the next day but when he awoke he found himself sleeping on his mother's front door step with the treasure chest beside him. Jonathan's mother opened the door and was overjoyed to see her son.

"Where have you been?" she asked.

"If I tell you, Mummy, you will never believe me," Jonathan replied with a sly smile.

CHAPTER 3

JONATHAN AND THE SEA MONSTER

One day when Jonathan went to visit his friend the pretty mermaid that lived in the blue hole he found her crying.

"Why are you crying?" Jonathan asked softly.

"I am crying because I am so lonely. I miss my family, especially my sisters,"

"Well, why don't you go and visit them?" Jonathan asked.

"Because they live far away in the deep ocean and I am afraid to travel there for fear that I will be eaten by the giant sea monster. That is why I have lived here in this blue hole all by myself for many years. The underwater tunnel that led to the ocean from the blue hole was closed by an earthquake and I cannot return that way. I will have to travel across land to the coast and then swim across many seas to my home," the mermaid sobbed.

"Don't worry" Jonathan replied. "I will take you across the land and to the coast but I cannot join you in the sea because I cannot breathe under water for very long,"

Jonathan said sadly.

"I can cast a spell that will allow you to breathe under water just like me. The spell will last for seven days but that is more than enough time for you to help me to return home," the mermaid told Jonathan. Jonathan agreed.

After gathering all the weapons that the mermaid had hidden in the blue hole, she and Jonathan started their journey across land. Jonathan used a wheel barrel to push the mermaid to the coast. When they arrived at the coast, the mermaid cast the spell and they entered the sea.

Jonathan was fascinated by his ability to swim under water and not have to come up for air. He was amazed at the beautiful sea world. His mother always told him that Andros had the third largest barrier reef in the world but the sight of the coral took his breath away. The corals were in many different shapes and colors. The Brain coral and the Staghorn coral and Sea fans were mesmerizing. The purples, blues, oranges and gold were fascinating. Little fish like the Surgeon fish and the Clown Trigger fish swam between the coral and the ray of sunlight made it appear like an enchanting new world. The sponges, sea urchins, jellyfish, starfish and sea cucumbers looked like they were arranged there by an artist. Jonathan now knew why they called the Great Barrier Reef, the "Rainforest of the Ocean."

Before long Jonathan and the mermaid came across a giant sea turtle. The Androsians called this kind of sea turtle a loggerhead. The loggerhead tried to eat the pretty mermaid but Jonathan took his net and wrapped it around the loggerhead. As he was about to use his spear to kill the loggerhead, the loggerhead shouted

"Please don't kill me; I am not the sea monster!"

"If you are not the sea monster then why did you try to eat my friend, the pretty mermaid?" Jonathan asked angrily.

"I mistook her tail for that of a fish, I am sorry and I will not hurt your friend. Please let me go!" the loggerhead pleaded.

"Why should I let you go?" asked Jonathan. "Because if you let me go, I will help you slay the sea monster," the loggerhead replied.

Jonathan agreed. So Jonathan, the pretty mermaid and the loggerhead continued on their journey.

Before long, the trio came upon a giant stingray. As the pretty mermaid swam over the sand where the stingray was hiding, the stingray lashed out at her with his poisonous tail. The mermaid screamed and Jonathan and the loggerhead came rushing to her rescue. The loggerhead circled the stingray distracting him and Jonathan took his net and throws it over the stingray. Just as Jonathan was about to spear the stingray, the stingray shouted

"Please don't kill me; I am not the sea monster!"

"If you are not the sea monster then why did you try to eat my friend, the pretty mermaid?" Jonathan asked angrily.

"I mistook her tail for that of a fish and I thought she wanted to eat me. I am sorry I will not hurt your friend. Please let me go!" the stingray pleaded. "Why should I let you go?" Jonathan asked.

"Because if you let me go, I will help you to slay the sea monster," the stingray replied. Jonathan agreed. So Jonathan, the pretty mermaid, the loggerhead and the stingray continued on their journey.

Before long the group of four was in the deep ocean. The water was as blue as topaz and very deep. Then, they heard the mermaid scream. A gigantic shark was swimming fast behind her, snapping as he pursued. The loggerhead circled the shark to distract him while the stingray used his tail to whip the shark.

Jonathan took his harpoon and aimed for the shark. The harpoon got him in the tail. Jonathan then grabbed the net and threw it around his body so he will not swim off. As Jonathan was about to spear the shark in the middle section, the shark shouted "Please don't kill me; I am not the sea monster!" "Well, if you are not the sea monster then why did you try to eat my friend, the pretty mermaid?" Jonathan asked angrily.

"I mistook her tail for that of a grouper and I thought she would make a nice meal. But now I realize that she is a mermaid and I am very sorry. I will not hurt your friend. Please let me go!" begged the shark.

"Why should I let you go?" Jonathan asked. "Because if you let me go, I will help you slay the sea monster," replied the shark.

Jonathan agreed and the group of five continued on their journey.

After a while the sea got very rough and the group realized that a storm was passing over. They decided to take shelter in a sunken submarine.

Jonathan's mother had told him many stories of submarine that had appeared off the coast of Love Hill. Grandpa Roy had also told him the story when his vessel "The Adeline" sailed right over a submarine. The group felt very cosy and safe inside the submarine and there they waited until it was safe to come out. After a while, the group exited the submarine and was about to go to the surface when they saw it. The giant sea monster came toward them with its mouth gaping wide. It had eight legs and each was loaded with tentacles. The mermaid screamed, the turtle screamed, the stingray screamed, the shark screamed but

Jonathan shouted," Don't be afraid. We can kill this sea monster!" If we work together as a team, we candefeat it!"

With these words of encouragement the team began to attack the sea monster.

The sea monster was a giant Octopus and legend had it that the monster could devour schools of fish, whole sharks, huge sperm whales and full-grown manatees. It was also responsible for sinking many

ships as they sailed the waters between the out islands and New Providence. Jonathan's Grandpa, Captain Roy had told him about a dreadful encounter with such an Octopus.

The Octopus grabbed the pretty mermaid with one of its tentacles and was moving her toward his open mouth. The loggerhead circled around the monster to distract it but the monster grabbed the loggerhead in another tentacle. The stingray began to whip the sea monster but it too was taken up with one of the tentacles. The shark grabbed onto one of the tentacles and began to bite. It was able to cut one of the tentacles with its razor like teeth but the monster soon grabbed it up into one of its tentacles. Jonathan then got his spear and threw it at the Octopus. The spear landed in the Octopus' head but he seemed to be unaffected. Jonathan then knew that he had to use his harpoon and shoot the creature in the eye. As Jonathan was about to harpoon the creature, the monster grabbed Jonathan up with one of its tentacles. However, Jonathan did not give up. He still tried to shoot the creature.

Then they heard sounds of shouts and screams. It was the entire mermaid nation. They had heard the screams of the pretty mermaid and they swam to her aid. There were hundreds of mermaids and mermen with swords and spears and they all began to attack the giant Octopus. As the monster tried to fight off an entire army, Jonathan aimed his harpoon and shot it right into the eye of the giant beast. The monster screamed in agony and fought ferociously. However, it was no good for the Octopus was subdued with the effort of the entire army. Afterwards they tied the monster up and dragged him away.

The pretty Mermaid was overjoyed to see her family and friends. She told them how Jonathan risked everything to bring her home. To show their gratitude for helping the pretty Mermaid, the King of the Mer people made Jonathan a national hero and granted him all the treasures he wanted. He also cast a spell that would allow Jonathan to swim under water as long as he liked, whenever he liked.

After a few days Jonathan returned home to Love Hill where he shared his latest adventure with his mother, father and his sister Jasmine.

CHAPTER 4

JASMINE AND THE TREE OF LIFE

Jasmine came home from school one day excited about what she had learnt in her history lesson. She raced to tell her mom. Her teacher had told them about the journal of Christopher Columbus in which he described a unique tree. Columbus said that the tree had one trunk but many different branches, but each branch was of a different type, with different leaves, different shapes, different sizes and different colors.

"Do you think the tree is real?" Jasmine asked her mother.

"Yes, the tree is real," Jasmine's mother replied.

"How do you know?" Jasmine pleaded.

"Because I heard about it when I was a little girl and the older women in the settlement have reported to have seen it," Jasmine's mother informed her. "I want to find that tree!" Jasmine shouted.

"It would be good if you did because it is believed that this tree could cure all illnesses. It is also believed to be the tree that the Arawaks used to cure sicknesses and to keep themselves well. This tree even cured the disease known as small pox which was brought to the new world by the white strangers," Jasmine's mother said.

"How can I find this tree?" Jasmine asked.

"You would have to seek out the oldest woman in each of these three settlements, Blanket Sound, Love Hill and Cargill Creek and convince them to tell you the location," Jasmine's mother informed her.

The next day, Jasmine went in search of the three old women. These women were known as the bush medicine women in their settlements and they helped to cure many ailments.

Jasmine went first to Blanket Sound where she found an old woman called "Teta" (Tet-ta). Teta was 119 years old but she looked as though she was in her late fifties. When Teta saw Jasmine coming, she began singing, Pretty gal, pretty gal whom do you seek,

I can teach you the right things you should eat.

"Teta, I would like to know where I can find the tree of life," Jasmine asked.

Teta laughed a wicked laugh a wicked laugh and then responded,

"Pretty gal I can only tell you the day you need to look for the tree as the tree is only visible for one day of the year," Teta replied.

"Will you tell me the day, please?" Jasmine pleaded.

"I will," Teta replied "but first you must spend one week with me and I will teach you all I know about bush medicine."
Jasmine agreed.

Jasmine spent seven days with Teta who showed her how to mix and make many home remedies. She told her how to boil the pear leaf and the Sour sop leaf and drink it as a tonic for high blood pressure. She also taught her how to use the Pawpaw to stop stomach gas and sour stomach.

She also taught her how to boil the leaves of the Yellow Elder to treat diabetes. She was also taught how to use the Aloe Vera to heal cuts and burns and to prevent internal infection and to clean the body and blood.

At the end of seven days Teta told Jasmine the day when the tree appeared. The tree appears only on the 13th day in the month. Jasmine thanked Teta for her help and continued her journey.

Jasmine's next stop was Love Hill where she found an old woman called "Dada" (Da-da). Dada was 115 years old but looked as though she was in her mid-fifties. When Dada saw Jasmine coming, she began to sing,

Pretty gal, pretty gal, come here to me,
Let me teach you about health mysteries.

"Pretty gal, I can only tell you the month you need to look for the tree as it appear for only one day in that month," Dada replied

"Will you tell me the month please?" Jasmine pleaded. "I will," Dada replied. "But first you must spend one week with me and I will teach you all I know about bush medicine."

"Dada, I would like to know where I can find the tree of life?" Jasmine asked respectfully.

Dada laughed a wicked laugh and responded,

Jasmine agreed.

Jasmine spent seven days with Dada who taught her how to boil the sweet Margaret to stop diarrhea and the Love vine as a health wash for hair and skin. She instructed her how to prepare the Shepherd's needle to reduce fever and relieve upset stomach.

As well as, how to use the Shepherd's needle to eliminate tapeworms in children and how to apply it to insect stings to reduce swelling.

At the end of the seven days Dada told Jasmine the month when the tree appeared. The tree appears only in the 10th month of the year and that would be the month of October. Jasmine thanked Dada and continued on her journey.

Jasmine's next stop was the settlement of Cargill Creek where she found an old woman called Meme (Mem-me). Meme was 102 years old but she looked like she was in her early fifties. When Meme saw Jasmine coming, she began to sing,

Pretty gal, pretty gal, listen to me,

These are the things that will keep you healthy. "Meme, can you tell me where I can find the tree of life?"

Meme laughed a wicked laugh and then responded. "Pretty gal, I can only tell you the place where you can find the tree of life as the tree only grows in one specific place." "Will you tell me the place, please?" Jasmine pleaded.

"I will," Meme replied, "But first you must spend one week with me and let me teach you all I know about bush medicine."

Jasmine agreed.

Jasmine spent seven days with Meme and she taught Jasmine all she knew about bush medicine. She taught her how the seeds of the Castor Oil plant can be dried, beaten and boiled into a pure oil laxative. It can also be used to treat asthma and the water from the leaves can be used to reduce the pain of arthritis. The oil can also be used on the skin to heal cuts, blemishes and burns. Jasmine was also taught how to use Cerasee to treat colds and flu and to reduce fever. She was also taught how to chop up the young coconut and mix it with the coconut water, boil it and use it to treat stomach aches.

At the end of seven days Meme told Jasmine the place where the tree could be found. "The tree grows only in the interior of Andros in the thick coppice. The tree can be found growing in a sink hole surrounding by many trees. The tree can only be seen when the Southeast and Northeast winds blow at the same time causing the Madeira, Mahogany, Madeira, one will be Horseflesh and one will be a Mahogany. You must not tie yourself to the Kamalami as it is the weakest of the trees and it will break under the force of the winds. After some time the winds will stop blowing for five minutes, you must then grasp this chance to pick all the leaves you can possibly pick and then tie yourself back to the trees before the winds start blowing again," Meme told Jasmine.

Jasmine thanked Meme for all her advice and then continued on her journey. She took with her a sturdy rope and a crab sack. The night before the 13th of October which was also Jasmine's birthday, Jasmine tied herself tightly to the Pine tree, Madeira, Horseflesh and Mahogany trees. She was careful not to use the Kamalami as she remembered Meme's warning. Horseflesh, Kamalami and Pine trees that surround it to bend. However, you must be careful not to be caught up in the wind because it will take you away forever," Meme told Jasmine.

"How can I stop myself from being blown away?" Jasmine asked.

"You must carry a sturdy rope and the night before the

The next day as the sun began to rise, the winds began to blow. As the winds blew, some of the trees bent to the West, some bent to the East, some bent to the North and some bent to the South. In the middle of all the trees in a very deep sink hole stood the Tree of Life, standing straight and unaffected by the winds. The winds made a terrible noise and it sounded like people crying, like dogs howling and like wood breaking. Jasmine was shocked at the beauty of the tree. She had never seen anything like it. The tree had one trunk but many branches. Each branch had a different set of leaves and the leaves were many different shapes and colors. Some were round shaped, others were oval shaped, some were smooth edged and others were rigid. Some were green in color, others were orange, gold, purple, brown and even yellow. tree is to appear you must tie yourself to the four strongest trees, one will be a Pine tree, one will be Jasmine waited until she heard the wind stop blowing and saw that the trees were no longer moving and she untied herself and hastily picked as many leaves as she could. When her sack was almost full, she quickly tied herself back to the trees. Then the winds began to blow. The winds blew hard and the trees that were bent went back to their original positions.

Soon the forest was closed again and there was no sight of the Tree of Life. When the winds stopped blowing, Jasmine untied herself and returned to Love Hill. Her mother was overjoyed to see her. She was also pleased when Jasmine showed her the sack of many different leaves. Jasmine became known as the medicine lady because she was able to cure all illnesses using the leaves from the Tree of Life.

CHAPTER 5

JONATHAN AND THE FIGHT FOR
THE PIRATE'S TREASURE

One day as Jonathan was going through one of his treasure chests, he came across an old tattered map. The map was a treasure map and it showed the location to the greatest pirate's treasure in the entire New World. Legend had it that when Governor Woodes Rogers came to The Bahamas in 1718, he offered all pirates a Royal pardon if they would give up their life of piracy. While most of the pirates accepted the offer, they had no intentions of giving up their gold, silver, pearls, diamonds and other forms of wealth. As a result they decided to load all their treasures in three huge ships and bury them on a deserted island known only to a select few.

Three pirates were given the location of the treasure and they were made to drink from the Creek of Youth so they would be the guardians of the treasure forever. The Creek of Youth was located somewhere in the Mangroves of Andros known as "Old House". Each of the three pirates were given a specific coordinate for locating the treasure but none of the pirates knew all three coordinates. The pirates had planned to trick Woodes Rogers and pretend to change and become model citizens but after three years they planned to meet at High Cay, off the Coast of Andros to share the spoils. As a result, they would be able to convince the settlers that they had gained their wealth lawfully. However, things did not go as the pirates had planned and many of them were executed before the three years were up, a few died of natural causes and some were marooned on islands and left for dead. Those who did not suffer any of the fate above died of the disease that hit the islands - cholera.

Jonathan wanted to find more information on this pirate's treasure and so he went to Grandpa Roy who knew about many of the legends concerning pirates. Grandpa Roy assured Jonathan that the legend was true but it would be difficult for him to find the treasure because he would have to first find the three guardians of the treasure and defeat all three of them in a battle.

"What if I can't defeat them?" Jonathan asked.

"Then you would have to make a pact with the pirate. To make a pact with the pirate you would have to tell the pirate his name and get him to plead allegiance to you?" Grandpa Roy told Jonathan.

"How will I know the pirates' name?" asked Jonathan. "You would have to find the list of all the pirates who were on board the three ships in 1718, find out which pirates took the pardon, which died of natural diseases, which died of cholera and which were executed and then you would be able to detect which three were left as guardians to the treasure," Grandpa Roy told Jonathan.

"How can I find the names of all of the pirates who were on board those three ships?" Jonathan asked. "Well, you will have to search the archives and find out the names of all the pirates that frequented The Bahamas around those times and find out which ships they sailed under and whose command. I can tell you the captains of these three ships. Their names were Captain Blackbeard, Captain Calico Jack, and Captain Blood. Now all you have to do is find out all the names of their crew members", Grandpa Roy explained.

Jonathan could not wait to go to the Library where he researched all the pirates who sailed with those three captains. After a few days he had a list of more than ninety men and women who helped to pillage the seas. He then went and searched all the prison and death records to find out who was executed, who died of cholera and who died of natural causes. After a few days he was left with four names. He knew the three guardians had to be three of the four persons, but how will he identify them. He then searched the stories that were told about each of the pirates to find out how each looked (whether they had scars, height, weight and other her physical attributes).

He also researched the type of weapon they liked and their particular fighting styles. After many weeks of research, Jonathan was sure he was ready to challenge the pirates. But like before any adventure, he went to his Grandpa Roy for advice.

"Do you really think you can defeat the three guardians?" Grandpa Roy asked.

"Yes, Grandpa, I am ready!" Jonathan responded. "Remember, these pirates were chosen because they were the best fighters and the cruelest of all the pirates. They can wheel an axe or hatchet and handle a sword better than most people can handle a spoon. Before you go, I will like for you to spend three weeks with my friend, karate Master Shang, who will teach you how to use the weapons from your treasure chest and show you some martial arts," said Grandpa. Jonathan agreed.

Jonathan spent three weeks with Master Shang and learnt all he could. After which Jonathan gathered up all his weapons, three weeks supply of food and with the precious map got in his canoe and rowed to his first destination. The map had indicated that the three guardians would be living on three different Cays off the East coast of Andros. The three Cays were Pigeon cay, Gaulin Cay and Goat Cay. Jonathan went first to Pigeon Cay. He knew he had arrived at the right cay because a flock of pigeons flew over his head the moment he arrived on the beach.

Jonathan exited his canoe and set up his tent on the beach. He had only been there for one day when he saw a pirate coming across the sand.

The pirate was tall with long, black hair. He had a moustache and a beard. His eyes were as red as blood and his skin was as rough as an alligator's. He had a pipe sticking out of his mouth and he ranked of tobacco and rum. He wore long gold earrings in each ear and a long gold earring in his nose. He wheeled two swords, one in each hand. Around his waist was a belt which held two pistols. His teeth were stained yellow from the tobacco and the expression on his face was meant to intimidate.

As the pirate approached Jonathan began to have second thoughts about fighting for the pirate's treasure. I really don't need this treasure, Jonathan thought to himself. I am already wealthy, maybe I should jump in my canoe and head for home. Na! I came for the thrill of the fight. Before Jonathan could complete his thoughts, the pirate shouted

"Why are you on my cay?"

"I have come to fight you and make you tell me where the pirate's treasure can be found!" Jonathan roared. The pirate laughed "Ha! Ha! Ha! You fight me, Are you crazy?"

"I can defeat you with one eye closed!" Jonathan echoed. Jonathan tried to be brave by pushing out his chest and clutching to his sword.

"Well, I have not had a good fight in almost three hundred years and I think I am going to enjoy this. Well young lad, lets begin!"

"Bring it on!" Jonathan shouted.

Jonathan and the pirate began to fight. The pirate ran into Jonathan with his sword and Jonathan retaliated, strike for strike. Master Shang had taught Jonathan well and he was able to flip while using his sword and maneuvered his body to avoid hits. The pirate pulled out a second sword and so did Jonathan. The sound of metal hitting metal was terrifying and for a while it would seem that the two was so equally matched that they could not defeat each other. Then, the pirate did a dirty trick and pulled out his pistol and fired at Jonathan. But because the pistol had not been fired in almost three hundred years it misfired sending the pirate flying to the ground. The pirate was out cold. Jonathan grasped the opportunity to tie him to a tree and then he splashed him with a bucket of salt water. When the pirate awoke, he was angry that he had been defeated.

"How can a whim like you defeat me, the greatest pirate on the seas?" the pirate roared.

"I have news for you, piracy is no more, all pirates are dead and the seas are no longer as you remember them!" Jonathan replied.

"What about all my mates who pillaged the seas with me? Are they all dead?" the pirate asked.

"That's what I said" Jonathan replied. You might a well tell me where I can find the Pirate's treasure and I will share some of it with you?" "I never will, I swore the pirate's oath," replied the pirate.

"I know you did, but that oath can be broken, if I tell you your name," Jonathan informed the pirate. "That is correct lad, well tell me my name?" insisted the pirate.
"Your name is John Joseph Newton III a.k.a. "Johnnie two swords," Jonathan said.

"How did you know?" asked the pirate. "Simple, Jonathan replied, "You fight with two swords."
Therefore, Johnnie two swords told Jonathan what he knew about the pirate's treasure. To locate the treasure, you must find the old lighthouse that is in the Fresh Creek Harbor. From the door

of the old light house you must walk 100 yards to the SOUTHEAST and mark your point with a stake. When you get the other two coordinates from the other two pirates, the coordinate will form a triangle. The treasure will be located in the Centre of the triangle," the pirate told Jonathan.

"How do I know you are telling the truth?" Jonathan asked.

"You have my word as a pirate, Ha! Ha! Ha! And since you have defeated me fair and square in a duel, you also have my loyalty, I am at your service," the pirate bowed to Jonathan.

So Jonathan and the pirate enjoyed a hearty meal of roasted pigeons and a good night's rest because they knew they had a long journey ahead of them.

The next day the pair climbed into Jonathan's canoe and sailed for Gaulin Cay. They knew they had arrived at the correct Cay because it was swarming with Gaulins. Jonathan was annoyed by the noise but Johnnie two swords told him that the birds made nature come alive and that they were very tasty too. As the pirate barbecued some Gaulin over an open fire, Jonathan decided to go and explore the cay. When Jonathan reached the other side of the cay, he heard a rushing sound and then he felt it. It was the feel of a booth in his back as he fell to the ground. He looked up to see a female pirate standing over him. Her booth was firmly situated in Jonathan's chest. The pirate looked like an Amazon woman for she was as big and strong as a man. She had a long crooked nose that looked as though it had been broken a couple of times. Her hair must have been naturally blonde but it was bleached white from exposure to the sun. Her hair was thick and unkept and filled with tangles and sand and twigs from the trees. She wheeled a hatchet in her right hand and a rope in her left hand. It looked as though Jonathan's worst nightmare had come true.

"Why are you on my Cay?" shouted the pirate.

"I want you to tell me how to find the pirate's treasure!" Jonathan replied.

"Not in this century" the pirate replied.

"I challenge you to a duel!" Jonathan exclaimed.

"A duel, HA! Ha! Ha!" the pirate laughed. I may be a woman but you are no match for me. I fought with Blackbeard and Calico Jack and none of them wanted a piece of me! I can defeat you in less time that it takes me to comb my hair!"

"Well, looks like that will take about all day because your hair has not been combed in almost three hundred years.

You look like you can use a haircut. I promise you that after I have defeated you, I will grant you one," Jonathan said with a laugh.

These words angered the pirate and she threw her hatchet and began to fight. The hatchet missed Jonathan and went flying through the air. Jonathan was quicker and faster than she was and was out of the way in a jiffy. He was taught well by Master Shang and as he flipped over her head he gave her a little slap. This angered the pirate more and she began to use profanity.

"Now, that's not ladylike. You should watch your mouth!" Jonathan said sarcastically.

"And you should watch your head!" the pirate shouted as she wheeled a second hatchet.

Jonathan jumped out of the way and the hatchet went flying into the trunk of a casuarina tree. She then began to use her rope. She wheeled it in the air like a lasso and then tried to throw it around Jonathan but she missed. The third time she caught him around the legs, and then she tried pulling him to her. She realized that Jonathan was too strong and so she grabbed her pistol, aimed it at Jonathan and fired. But because the pistol was not fired in almost three hundred years, the only thing that came out of it was smoke. The black smoke got into the pirate's eyes and she scrambled about like a chicken. In her scrambling she fell over a log and was out cold. Jonathan grasped the opportunity to tie her to a tree and then took delight in splashing her with cold water to wake her up. The pirate awoke screaming,

"Untie me, you scalawag!"

"Not until you tell me your coordinates to the pirates' treasure!" replied Jonathan.

"I cannot tell you because I have taken the pirate's oath!" the pirate said.

"That oath can be broken if I tell you your name," Jonathan informed her.

"Well, scalawag, what is my name?" insisted the pirate. "Your name is Jane Rackham a.k.a. Hatchet Jane," Jonathan said with a smile. "Now will you tell me your coordinates and allow me to make you a very rich woman, then you can buy all the combs in the world, heaven knows you are going to need them!"

"All right!" hatchet Jane replied. "Since you have defeated me fair and square in a duel, I will tell you my coordinates. You also have my loyalty as I am at your service!" said the female pirate, as she bowed down to Jonathan. As a result, Hatchet Jane told Jonathan the coordinates to the treasure. When you find the stake from the first coordinates given by the first pirate you must walk fifty feet to the SOUTH and mark your stake.

"How do I know you are telling the truth?" Jonathan asked the pirate.

"Because you have my word as a pirate said Hatchet Jane as she smiled a wicked smile. Besides I am tired of being on this cay all by myself, I am ready to continue my pillaging of the seas!" she exclaimed. "Well, I've got news for you, the days of piracy are over and women are now respectable ladies. You can use some of the riches from the pirate's treasure to buy yourself a nice mansion and live the life of a princess, even though I know being a princess is going to be hard for you!" Jonathan laughed.

"You are a terrible, terrible scalawag!" shouted Hatchet Jane.

Jonathan untied Hatchet Jane and took her back to the beach where Johnnie Two Swords was waiting with barbecued Gaulin. The two were happy to see each other and they laughed as they embraced. Jonathan shared with Hatchet Jane bottles of the most expensive cologne from his treasure chest and she could not stop thanking him. After a long night of talking and sharing adventures the trio went to sleep because they knew they had a long journey ahead of them.

The next morning the trio headed for Goat Cay. The cay seemed deserted and there seemed to be very little wild life on the Cay.

While Johnnie Two Swords and Hatchet Jane talked about the good old days, Jonathan decided to explore the island.

When Jonathan got to the other side of the Cay, he saw the only goat on the entire Cay. The goat seemed to be trapped in a net. As he was about to untie the goat, he heard a rough voice ask,

"Why are you on my Cay? Did you come to eat my goat?"

Jonathan turned around to see the most terrifying figure he had ever seen.

The pirate was a mulatto but his skin was burnt black from the hot sun. He wore his hair in Rasta plaits and they hung all the way down to his waist.

On each of his Rasta plaits was a tooth of an animal tied to it. He wore goat skins on his arms and legs. He even had on goat skin booths.

He had the skull of a goat tied to his left shoulder and his fingernails were as long as pencils. He had a cutlass tied to his left side and a musket to his right side. He wheeled a machete in his left hand and a file in his right.

"No! I do not want to eat your goat. I will like for you to tell me your coordinates to the pirate's treasure!" Jonathan replied.

The pirate looked at Jonathan as he sharpened his machete, "Ha! Ha! Ha!" the pirate laughed. "Did you bring the King's army or navy with you? Because that is what you are going to need to make me tell you my coordinates," the pirate shouted.

"King, King! There is no more King. There isn't even a Kingdom. The days of piracy are gone and everyone tries to live an honest and descent life!" Jonathan informed the pirate.

"Are you saying that I am not descent and honest?" the pirate said sarcastically

"Well, you are a Pirate," Jonathan replied. 'Pirates are not without honor. We have rules by which we abide. Our word is our bond and on my word I will let you have my last goat if you defeat me in a duel!"

"This cay is called Goat Cay, why is there only one goat left?" Jonathan asked.

"Because I have eaten them all!" laughed the pirate. "However, you have my word that I will not eat you, not unless I get very hungry!" the pirate growled.

With those words, Jonathan knew he had to defeat the pirate. It was a pity that he had come alone and did not have Johnnie Two Swords and Hatchet Jane to help him. Jonathan threw his sword and launched at the pirate but the pirate was quick on his feet. He maneuvered the machete as if it was a part of his own arm. He was bigger than Jonathan and Jonathan could feel the extraordinary strength of the pirate every time his machete hit Jonathan's sword. Jonathan knew he had met his match.

Jonathan used every move that Master Shang taught him but he could not defeat the pirate and then the unthinkable happened, Jonathan slipped in the sand. Jonathan thought his end had come and pictures of his mother, father, sister Jasmine and Grandpa Roy flashed before him.

Just as the pirate was about to strike Jonathan with the machete, the goat came running up from behind the pirate and bucked him in the buttocks. The pirate went crashing to the ground. As he was about to get up, the goat bucked him again, this time in the head and the pirate was out cold.

Jonathan took this opportunity to tie up the pirate making sure that he could not move a muscle. He then got some salt water and threw it on the pirate to wake him up. When the pirate woke up, he was angrier than ever.

"You did not defeat me fair and square, you must untie me and we will fight again!" shouted the pirate.

"I don't think so," Jonathan replied. "If you tell me the coordinates to the pirate's treasure, I will take you to a place where you can have all the goats you like for the rest of your life" Jonathan told the pirate.

"You call that a bargain? You will have to offer me more than that!" the pirate shouted.

"Well I can leave you here, tied to this tree and you can watch as I take your last goat away. Imagine yourself dying of starvation!" Jonathan said wickedly.

"Enough! Enough!" the pirate yelled. "I will tell you what you want to know but first you must release me from my pirate's oath by telling me my name!" "Well!" Jonathan replied. "Your name is James Jenson a.k.a. Machete Jenson.

"How did you know my name was Machete Jenson and not Machete Johnson?" the pirate asked.

"Simple, Machete Johnson hated red meat and would only eat chicken. There is no way he would have let the other pirates leave him on Goat Cay!" Jonathan said.

"Clever lad, now untie me!" shouted the pirate.

"Not until I have the coordinates!" Jonathan insisted.

Therefore, Machete Jenson told Jonathan his coordinates to the pirate's treasure.

When you find the second stake marked by the second pirate, then you must walk 150 yards Northwest and back to the door of the old lighthouse. When all three coordinates are in then you must put a level through all three points and dissect it dead in the Centre. In the Centre is where you should dig for the treasure," said the pirate.

"How do I know you are telling me the truth?" Jonathan asked.

"You have my word as a Pirate!" the pirate laughed. Jonathan knew he had to take the pirate at his word, so he untied him and together with the goat they returned to the twosome on the beach. Johnnie Two Swords and Hatchet Jane were delighted to see Machete Jenson and they laughed as they embraced. Then they ate, drank and shared old stories. That night Jonathan treated the group to a wonderful meal of mutton which he brought with him. He would not let anyone touch the goat because he was indebted to him. They went to bed early because they were all eager to begin their search for the pirates' treasure.

The next day the foursome got up early and piled into Jonathan's canoe, their destination: the old light house at Fresh Creek Harbor. When they arrived at the site, Johnnie two swords set his coordinates and marked his point. Then Hatchet Jane set her coordinates and marked her point, and then Machete Jones set his coordinates and marked his point. Jonathan then squared up all of the coordinates and found the Centre. When the Centre was located, Jonathan marked it with a big X. After which they all got shovels and began to dig.

They were digging for what seemed like hours when the first shovel hit wood. After that, they were bringing up boxes and boxes of treasure. It took the foursome the entire day to unearth all the treasure. Then the task of sharing it came. The three pirates looked at each other and then at Jonathan and then Jonathan remembered Grandpa Roy's words

"Once a pirate, always a pirate".

CHAPTER 6

JASMINE AND THE JOURNEY TO THE SEA

I sat in one of the classrooms surrounded by the noise of my classmates. It was third period and my class had Mr. Cartwright for General Science. Everyone hated this subject and most of us found the classroom too hot to think. The boys were shouting at the top of their voices and picking on the girls they did not like. The girls were gossiping about each other and of course about boys. I was doing what I did best when I was bored, daydreaming.

Then out of the clear blue someone suggested that we go down to the beach. Suddenly there was a perfect silence as all eyes stared at Mr. Cartwright, the ball was now in his court. Mr. Cartwright shook his head in disagreement, then the ninth grade, which was considered one of the most intelligent group of students ever assembled together, began to use psychology, logic and blackmail.

"Please Mr. Cartwright, it is almost time for school to close and we have worked so hard, we deserve some fun!" exclaimed Henry, the class bully.

"Yes, Mr. Cartwright lets go to the beach" begged Evelyn, the girl with the baby face.

"Mr. Cartwright, if you don't take us to the beach we goin' make noise all day and we ain't goin' do no work!" threatened Leroy, the toughest of us all. There were moans and pleas throughout the entire class and then without a second thought I spoke. "Mr. Cartwright, my father has a road cut that leads straight to the beach; we could take that as a short cut. We could use this as a scientific field trip because we can explore the fauna and flora of Andros, the marsh land, the scrub land, the mangroves and all the different ecosystems.

We can examine how the animals relate to the ecosystem and to each other. I would like to discover how the guppies come to live in the ponds and only for a certain time each year. I had a theory that the crabs were responsible for bringing the guppies there. Now I knew that speaking like that would get Mr. Cartwright thinking. There were echoes of agreement from among the class.

Now, I lived about two hundred meters from the school on the left side of the Queen's Highway. Living on the left side simply meant that my home was on the Eastern side of the island near the coast. Being an explorer by nature, I knew almost everything about the back of my yard. I was familiar with scrub land, the swamp land, the mangroves, the blue holes, the ponds, the terrain and all types of vegetation. I knew about the special orchids that were only found on Andros Island. The only thing I did not know was how to get to the beach from the school as I had never walked the tract road made by my father but I was convinced that it could not be so bad.

Mr. Cartwright looked at me and then at all the other sympathetic faces and with a nod, he agreed. Mr. Cartwright was a British teacher who took his work very seriously and seemed to love perfection. A simple nod meant that he was in good spirits. With victorious shouts we filed out of the classroom, across the school yard toward my house, our destination: the beach.

The group which consisted of twenty four-eager minded students tiptoed across the slippery rocks, pass ponds, water holes and onto the tract road. The tract was narrow and only one person could pass at a time, naturally I took the lead.

As I parted the trees I was just as amazed as my classmates at the beauty of the Mahogany, Cedar, and Buttonwood trees but I pretended not to be impressed. The path had been made using a machete and the trees had begun to grow back, nevertheless, my friends were very impressed and I heard them shout to me

"Hey! Jasmine, this road ain't so bad you know! I did not reply or bother commenting for I was too busy using my body as a machete to make the path clearer for those who followed me. After walking for about ten minutes I realized that the path had come to an end but I was embarrassed to tell my classmates and my teacher, who thought so highly of me that we were lost. I did not panic because I was very accustomed to rambling and besides, I was sure that the beach could not be far. At that point a flock of sea gulls flew over our head heading East, "See there!" I said pointing to the birds. "You know wherever seagulls are the beach cannot be far?" This encouraged my adventurous classmates for a short while. By this time, my hands and legs were scratched and I was bleeding. My skin was also burning where the briars had scraped me. I did not complain but took special care to protect my face from the trees and branches as I thought I was pretty and could not bear to have any scars.

After about another three minutes which seemed like hours, my classmates noticed that the bushes had gotten thicker, the foot path had disappeared and the tract had taken on a number of twists and turns. Even the least intelligent in the group sensed something was wrong and she began to ask questions.

"Jasmine when we goin' to reach man?" asked Sally, one of the mean girls.

"Soon!" I echoed back.

Their constant nagging was beginning to unnerve me but then I noticed that some of the trees had a peculiar red mark on them which made them appear to have been sprayed. Cunningly, I decided to use this to my advantage.

"See that tree over there? I remember my daddy sprayed that red paint there the last time we came through here," I told my classmates.

The sight of the red marks on the trees made the group feel more secure.

By this time I was feeling like Christopher Columbus and I wondered what my classmates would do to me if they found out that I was lying. I could feel the tension and anxiety that was building up and silently I began to pray.

"Oh Lord, please help me to find the beach." Unknowingly, I rambled Southeast instead of directly East which made the journey much longer. I heard mumblings and moans of distress behind me and then I felt it. A cool breeze blew over us and I was convinced that we could not be far from the sea. I heard Donna, one of my closest friends say,

"Oh Jasmine, I feel the breeze, that mean we soon reach."

I shouted back to her,

"Yeah girl, just a Lil whiles more na!"

I kept walking, pushing my body through the thick trees, my limbs were all scratched with briar and they began to bleed even more. I heard the "cute" girls in the class complain about their appearance and I felt a sting of pleasure because I was not too fond of them anyway. I was also glad that I had taken the lead and so my classmates could not see the worried expression on my face and because I felt the tears in my eyes, I never looked behind.

We walked on for another five minutes, it could have been less but my imagination was running wild and my heart was pounding in my chest. The trees got shorter and thicker and the rocks became slippery. The water holes which contained crabs and fish seemed to be everywhere so there was hardly any place to walk. By this time my classmates had gotten so restless that they began to argue among themselves. "Walk up girl, you too cute! I wish you fall right down in one of these holes, see if I wouldn't walk over ya!" threatened one of the boys.

"Boy moo outa my way!" screamed one of the bully girls.

"Ouch! This bush hit me in my face!" screamed Sandra.

"Gees Jasmine when we goin' to reach?" I was certain that voice belonged to Leroy, the most complaisant person I have ever known, thus something was definitely wrong. I knew I was in trouble. If Columbus thought he was facing a mutiny then he should try trading places with me.

"Jasmine if I don't see the beach very soon then I am going to turn back!" shouted Leroy.

"Yeah and we going with him!" shouted Henry. "You sure you know where you are going Jasmine?" asked Sandra.

"Of course she knows where we going, she is the smartest girl in the class you know!" replied Donna, my very good friend.

Maybe we should sing a song, I shouted to the group and so I began.

Over the scrub land, over the marshland, over the swampland

We journey to the sea.

Over the Rock land, over the pond land, over the dry land

We journey to the sea.

Before long, the entire class had picked up on the chorus and we were all singing and laughing and enjoying being young and carefree. Then my worst nightmare came true. I came face to face with a cluster of trees and scrubs that were humanely impossible to penetrate. Coupled with my fear and the nagging of my classmates, I swung around with so much force that I almost fell of my feet. As our eyes met, I searched their eyes for reassurance but there wasn't any, they searched my eyes for answers but they were too blurry. Then I confessed in one straight sentence, "I might as well brief you all, I don't know where we goin!"

At first there was complete silence as everyone tried to digest what I had just said. Then in a tantalizing moment it happened. Everything went wrong. Everyone started screaming and running in all four directions. I stood stunned as I watched a group of boys tear through the scrubs that I had thought impossible to penetrate. The so-called ladies seemed to have forgotten their femininity as they raised their gown tails and imitated the actions of the boys which were in no way ladylike. Profane language was escaping from the lips of the most respected students and the sounds of clothing being ripped echoed through the air. There was no show of brotherly love. The motto was every man for himself and God for us all.

With that realization, I looked around for Mr. Cartwright only to find that he too had ran off. After that I panicked and curtailed behind the nearest person who happened to be the fattest girl in the class. I watched as she stooped down and went under a huge fallen tree trunk. I was about three times smaller than she was and so I thought if she could do it, I could do

it to. I mimicked her actions but in my hurry to catch up with the others I ascended too quickly. I heard a screeching noise and ascended to find that my blouse had been torn straight down the back and now lay like a shoal about my body.

When I finally caught up with my peers, I noticed that the boys who could swim had swam across the mangroves onto the beach but the girls accompanied with Mr. Cartwright had proceeded in walking up the scrub. Mr. Cartwright called everyone by name to be sure that everyone was accounted for. When he finally reached to my name, I heard kissing of teeth and profanity.

We had to walk the scrub up to the beach road and then follow the beach road onto the main highway. This highway led us back to school which was about a two-mile walk in the scorching hot sun. We were all bruised, scratched, thirsty and tired. I walked behind the others who occasionally looked behind and shook threatening fists at me. When we arrived at the school all of the students and teachers came out to meet us. The ninth grade was not very popular because we were considered too sophisticated so those who didn't like us took the opportunity to have a good laugh on us. Some students actually came out of their classrooms, pointed at us and fell to the ground with laughter.

To my surprise, neither my classmates nor Mr. Cartwright asked me for an apology or an explanation; however, whenever I suggested that we do something they were quick to disagree. The incident became a nightmare that no one wanted to remember.

Almost exactly a year later, my brother Jonathan and my cousins, James, Jariska, Janeice, Jaiden, Tristan, Tyler, Davidvivo and TK and I started out on the same journey, our destination: the beach. This time however, we were prepared and wore suitable protective clothing. We carried machetes to help pave the way. Jonathan knew of my previous adventure and therefore I was urged to stay in the rear.

After about thirty minutes of walking, chapping and arguing we became restless. My younger cousins had grown restless and suggested that we turn back but Jonathan refused to quit.

"We will find the beach even if it takes us the rest of our lives!" Jonathan exclaimed.

After more chapping and murmuring among ourselves of who was right and who was wrong, we finally reached the mangroves. The black and red mangroves looked frightening but we knew we had to cross over them; it was either do or die. Fortunately, tide was low and the tallest among us was able to cross with the water reaching our chest. The shorter ones were carried across on the backs of the taller ones.

When we emerged from the thick casuarina and first sighted the sea, our hearts filled with joy. My cousins raced across the glittering sand and into the sea, but I stooped down and kissed the sand. When I ran into the sea, I noticed something big and dark coming toward me, it was a gigantic shark. I ran out of the sea screaming at the top of my voice, "SHARK! SHARK! SHARK!"

I watched as my cousins raced out of the water. They all looked at me with gratitude in their eyes. We all walked the beach in silence to the beach road and then home.

Today, I wonder why I imitated Columbus in kissing the sand. Columbus's rediscovery had introduced Europe to different races, to riches, to navigational knowledge and to a new world. What did I discover? Was it fear or was it just a beach? I feel that in those two journeys I discovered something greater than fear or land. I had discovered a driving force, a determination to succeed, a strong belief and a fearless spirit that is within all of us, it certainly was in Christopher Columbus and it was definitely inside of me.

CHAPTER 7

JONATHAN AND THE GREEN MILANDER

"They found him! They found him!" Jonathan screamed.

"Found who?" Jonathan's mother asked.

Jonathan was so excited that he could hardly speak. He had run a straight mile to tell his mother the good news.

"They found Mr.Toadler!" Jonathan replied.

Mr.Toadler was an elderly man who lived in Love Hill and went fishing and crabbing for a living. The people of the village always knew where to get fresh fish even when the weather was bad. Mr.Toadler also supplied the villagers with crabs even after the season was over.

He was the best crab digger in town. He was not afraid of snakes and other things that lived in the crab holes but whatever was in a hole he would pull it to the surface. Jonathan enjoyed talking to him and hearing about the times when he pulled huge foul snakes out of the crab holes.

Now the entire village was sad, because Mr.Toadler was missing for over a week. Mr. Toadler had gone crabbing and not returned. Some people believed he was eaten by alligators, or taken by Chickcharnie or may have fallen into a deep sink hole. Some of the old women were convinced that he was taken by the Jack Ma Lantern. A search party went out looking for him every day and some volunteers even went at night, but they came up empty. After the seventh day they found him.

"Where did they find him?" Jonathan's mother asked. "They found him in one of the dirt roads that leads to Twin Lakes. But there is something wrong with him," Jonathan replied.

"Something wrong with him? What do you mean?" Jonathan's mother asked with a concerned voice. "He seems to be talking out of his head. He told the police that he was taken by a huge green man who held him hostage and would not let him go. The nurse and the doctor said he must be dehydrated and delirious," Jonathan informed his mother.

"I don't think anything is wrong with him, I believe he saw what he saw," Jonathan's mother replied. Jonathan burst into a thunderous laugh "Ha! Ha! Ha!, Green men do not exist, he must have been dreaming, hallucinating or delirious like the doctor said," Jonathan said to his mother.

"Sit down Jonathan and I will tell you a story. When I was eleven years old, an old lady spotted an Iguana in the coppice. She called my father and uncle who took their guns and went after it. In those days the iguana meat was a rare treat and when caught the whole village would have a feast. Well, my father and uncle were chasing the iguana in the coppice and then I saw it. It was a tall green creature with the shape of a man but it was green and wore no clothing at all. It had no body hair and it had yellow eyes and yellow teeth. Its lips were as red as fire and its ears were pointed. It was running as fast as lighting but when it saw me, it looked at me for a split second. I could see that it was frightened because it thought that my father and uncle

were running after it. I thought it was the Iguana but when my father and uncle brought the iguana home I realized that what I saw was not an iguana at all but a strange creature that very few people have ever seen. The only other person who reported to have seen this creature was the old woman who called my father to shoot the iguana but the people called her crazy. My brother told me that I should never tell anyone of what I saw because they would call me crazy too. Now that Mr.Toadler has also seen the creature, I know that I saw what I saw," Jonathan's mother told her son.

For a while Jonathan was left speechless. He knew his mother would never lie to him and he knew if his mother said she saw something then he knew she did. He now believed that the creature existed, but what was it?

"What do you call the creature mother?" Jonathan asked a little frightened.

"I call it the Green Milander!" Jonathan's mother said with a whisper.

"I am going to find the Green Milander and take a picture!" exclaimed Jonathan.

"No, Jonathan, it's too dangerous. I don't know what the creature will do to you. Maybe some things are better left unknown. Let the creature be!"

For many days Jonathan could not take his mind off the Green Mainlander. He could not wait for Mr.Toadler to come out of the hospital to go and talk to him about the creature.

Mr.Toadler was happy to see Jonathan when he visited and was even happier to know that someone actually believed him.

He told Jonathan how the creature found him in a deep sink hole unable to get out but the creature rescued him and took him to his home deep in the coppice. He lived in a deep cave hidden by dense trees.

The cave had a flowing water supply and many caverns that went deep under the earth. .

The creature lived of berries, birds and wild boars but its favorite food was the iguana

He had many cages filled with iguanas of all sizes and he barbecued then over an open fire. The creature also had a cage filled with Hutias. Hutias looked like huge rats and was hunted by the Arawaks who stewed them in their favorite meal, pepperpot. The Milander must be the last of his kind because there were no signs of any other creatures living there. Mr.Toadler thought the creature was going to eat him and every day he planned his escape. The creature followed the same routine every day as so Mr.Toadler timed him and waited for the right moment to make his escape.

After talking with Mr.Toadler, Jonathan was even more determined to seek out the Green Milander. He convinced Mr.Toadler to tell him where the creature lived and then he began planning. He would take with him enough food to last for one week, good running shoes, long sleeved clothing, a cutlass, a search light and extra batteries and of course a loaded camera. After convincing his mother that he would be okay, (after all he slew the Harbor master, the sea monster and fought three pirates) he went with his mother's blessings.

The first day's journey was the easiest. Jonathan just followed the tracks that were made by the crabbers and pigeon shooters who frequented the white roads. By the second day the bushes became thicker and taller and by the third day he could hardly move anywhere without using his cutlass to chap through the dense under brush. When he got to the mangrove swamps, he became distraught. He had to walk through the boggy mud and was almost eaten alive by mosquitoes. He was always mindful of alligators and other swamp creatures but eventually he crossed the swamps and according to Mr.Toadler was in the creature's territory. He then saw a series of caves between the dense trees and decided to search them out. The first cave was a dead end and so he exited and entered a second. As he walked about in the second cave, he could hear water dripping. He walked over to an underground stream where he saw fish swimming. The fish looked like grunts, and snappers and Jonathan knew that his father would love to come fishing there. He was careful not to make any sudden movements as he noticed bats hanging upside down in the roof of the cave. The bats seemed to be asleep. Jonathan wondered if the bats were vampire bats. He also noticed centipedes and spiders moving about freely in the cave.

He then smelled something roasting on an open fire. He walked closer and shined his search light on it and saw that it was an iguana tied to a stick. He looked around but there was no sign of the Green Milander and so he decided to hide in a crack in the rock and wait for the creature to return. While hiding in the rock, Jonathan observed the stalactite that grew from the roof of the cave and the stalagmites that grew from the bottom. The limestone features were magnificent to look at.

The cave was so warm and comfortable and Jonathan was so tired that he did not know when he fell asleep. When the Green Milander returned he could smell that a human was in the cave. He went directly to the place where Jonathan was sleeping and stood over him. When Jonathan awoke, he saw the Green Milander staring down at him. Jonathan was frightened and tried to run but the creature crabbed him by the neck and lifted him up as if he was a piece of paper.

Jonathan wiggled and wiggled and tried to escape. The creature took Jonathan and threw him in one of the cages he used to keep the iguanas. Jonathan wished he had listened to his mother. The Green Milander took his time and went through Jonathan's belongings. He was fascinated with the search light and jumped about as the light shone throughout the cave. He took the cutlass and used it to chap some of the iguana meat of the barbecue rack. He seemed to be pleased with what the cutlass did and when he looked at Jonathan he smiled. His smile was scary enough to make Jonathan faint (big yellow teeth surrounded with red lips and green skin).

Jonathan remembered what his mother had told him " a smile is a smile in any language" and so he smiled back at the Green Milander.

After a while the Green Milander went over to the iguana and began to eat. He tore at the tough meat with his sharp teeth. Jonathan could tell that the meat was not completely done but it did not stop the Green Milander from enjoying his meal. After he finished eating the meat he went over to a spring and enjoyed a long drink. He then went over to a rock where the bones of flamingoes were stacked high. He took one, broke it into pieces and began to pick his teeth. Now Jonathan knew why there were no more flamingoes on Andros and very few iguanas, this monster had hunted and eaten them all. Jonathan wondered if the creature planned to eat him for breakfast or lunch or dinner. Nevertheless, he started to think of a plan to escape the Green Milander.

The next day when the Green Milander went out, Jonathan managed to escape from his cage, gathered his belongings and was about to leave went he spotted some drawings on the wall of the cave.

The drawings showed pictures of how the Milander came to be on Andros. It showed a flying saucer crashing in the mangrove swamps and an entire tribe of Milanders coming out of the space ship. It showed the tribe killing the flamingos, iguanas and wild boars and eating them as a way to survive. It showed that a disease came and killed out the entire tribe, leaving only one creature alive. Jonathan used his camera to take pictures of the strange writings and drawings on the wall of the cave but before he was through he heard the green Milander returning.

Jonathan turned just in time to take a picture of the creature and then he started to run. He remembered that his mother told him that the Milander was as fast as lightning and so he did not look back.

He ran as fast as he could but the Milander was too fast for him. The Green Milander ran through the trees as if they were not there. He jumped from tree to tree and then from branch to branch. He blended in with the trees as they were green and so was he. Jonathan only knew where he was from the movement of the branches and the sound of them breaking under the weight of the creature. After the greatest run of his life the Milander caught him by the arm but Jonathan swung his cutlass and the Milander let go for fear of losing its arm.

Jonathan was running and screaming at the same time and then he heard voices screaming back at him. A rescue team had come in search of Jonathan and he was relieved to see his fellow villagers.

Frightened by the large group of men, the Milander retreated into the forest. The villagers took Jonathan back to town and he was mumbling as he went " I saw the Green Milander, I saw the Green Milander!"

For many days Jonathan was sick with a high fever and everyone called him crazy. After he got well, he told his mother of his experience and his mother alone believed him. Then Jonathan remembered that he had taken pictures of the cave and the Green Milander. He rushed to have the pictures developed and then he shared them with the villagers. Everyone believed Jonathan and they all began to form search parties to find the Green Milander and capture him.

People came from far and wide to seek out the Green Milander but when they found the cave they discovered that the Milander had left. The Green Milander was never seen again but Jonathan and Mr.Toadler became very famous as everyone wanted to hear of their experiences with the Green Milander.

CHAPTER 8

JASMINE AND THE TAR BABY

"Race you up the hill!" Jonathan shouted to Jasmine.

"Catch me if you can!" Jasmine shouted back.

The two children dashed up the steep hill that led to their home. Jonathan was much faster than Jasmine but sometimes he let her win because she was his baby sister.

The children dashed into the yard where their mother was picking peas. The children's mother was proud of her yard. She grew pigeon peas, cassava, sweet potatoes, sugar cane, mangoes and bittersweet sour oranges right in the front of the yard. She also showed off a beautiful garden with every flower that could be found on Andros. She had what the old people called a knack for planting or a green thumb. "Jasmine, go and get a fanna and help me pick some peas, Jonathan go and feed the pig!" the mother instructed the children. As Jasmine helped her mother pick, the peas, they began to talk about the terrible situation that existed in the village. The people of the village used Tar babies to protect their fields from thieves and wild animals but a wild Tar baby had gotten away and was now attacking people. As a result no one was able to go into their fields for weeks and so there were no fresh field foods in the stores and at the marketplace. The children's mother was happy that she had her field in the front of her yard, and she will be able to cook her dumpling soup. The dumpling soup would have pigeon peas, beans, coconut milk, cassava, sweet potatoes, yams, eddies, whole corns, pumpkin, salt beef, ham, dried conch, flat dough, round dough and long dumplings. The children's father was looking forward to having dumpling soup when he came home from bone fishing.

"When do you think they will catch the Tar baby?" Jasmine asked her mother.

"I don't think they will ever catch the Tar baby because everyone is afraid, no one wants to be tarred. You know a tar baby can stick to you and take off all you skin. I once knew a man who got stuck to a tar baby and when we got the tar baby off him, he could no longer see and he needed plastic surgery to reconstruct his face. He also lost all the skin of his hands and arms and he could hardly walk after that!" Jasmine's mother said shaking her head in a sorrowful way. Jasmine was afraid but she was already thinking of her she could catch the Tar baby and become a hero like her brother Jonathan. The village people would be so proud of her and if she is injured by the tar baby she could always use the leaves she got from the Tree of Life to heal herself.

The next morning Jasmine got up very early, left a note on her pillar for her mother and headed out in search of the Tar baby. She had heard that the Tar baby was living in the fields and so she took the tract road that led to the fields. Very soon she came to a cross road and had to decide to take a left or right. At first she went left and came upon a corn field.

As she entered the sweet corn field she began to sing

Tar baby, Tar baby come out and play,

Come and play with me on a sunny day.

She saw no sign of the Tar baby. She then went into a cassava and sweet potato field and began to sing,

Tar baby, Tar baby come out and play,

Come and play with me on a sunny day.

She walked through the entire field singing her song but she saw no sign of the Tar baby. She decided to back track and then go right. She took the first field which was filled with pumpkins, water melons and cantaloupe but she saw no sign of the Tar baby. She decided to check one more field before returning home.

Before she entered the field, she stopped to drink from the water hole. She met a small iguana drinking there and so she waited until it was finished and then she took her turn. After she had drunk her fill, she climbed a dilly tree; picked a few of the biggest and ripest dillies she had ever seen and took her time in eating them. They were delicious and she was sure to save some of the seeds to carry home to her mother. She was singing very quietly,

Tar baby, Tar baby come out and play,

Come and play with me on a sunny day.

As she was still sitting in the tree, she heard a flock of birds fly away as if they were frightened. She then saw the little iguana running away, followed by the lizards and the snakes. Then she saw it, the Tar baby emerged from the dense trees and walked quietly through the field. The Tar baby was about six feet tall. It was jet black and tar dripped from its body. It had red blazing eyes that looked like fireballs. It had a big hole where the mouth should be and arms almost as long as its legs. In an effort to escape a bird flew too close to the Tar baby and stuck to its shoulder. The bird wiggled as it tried to brake away. The more the bird wiggled the more feathers came off the bird. Before long, the air was filled with bird feathers and the only thing that remained attached to the Tar baby was the bones of the bird. The Tar baby then took the bones and ate them. When Jasmine saw this, she gulped with fear and whispered to herself, "Run come see Jerusalem!" Maybe she should rethink her plan. Her first thought was to light the Tar baby afire but she realized that this could cause a bush fire which could burn down acres and acres of coppice, pine forest and fields. The fire would also kill many animals that are not fast enough to get out of its path. It could also kill many crabs as they lay hibernating in their holes. An unchecked fire in the coppice could cause more harm than good.

To destroy the Tar baby she knew that she had to lower it to the tar pit but she had to use herself as bait. She knew she was a fast runner, she had beaten Jonathan many times and Jonathan was the fastest runner in the entire village. Jasmine began talking to herself

"You can do this Jasmine, You can do it, you're fast, you're quick, and you're dangerous!"

"You can do this, you're fast, you're quick, and you're dangerous!"

"You can do this, you're fast, you're quick, and you're dangerous!"

Every time she repeated this, she became more confident. "You can do this, you're fast, you're quick, and you're dangerous!"

She repeated this four times, but the fourth time she said it so loud that the Tar baby heard her and looked up into the dilly tree. When Jasmine realized that the Tar baby had spotted her she jumped down out of the tree and began to run. She ran as fast as she could.

She was too afraid to look back but she could feel the tar baby on her heel. As she ran, she thought about her brother and she did not realize that she was calling his name out aloud, "Jonathan! Jonathan! Jonathan!" she shouted knowing that he could not hear her cries from miles away. Jasmine ran over the sharp edged rocks, she jumped over sinkholes in the road, she cut across fields, she even swung on the branches that were in her way. She knew where the tar pit was and the only thing she had to do was to get there before the Tar baby could get her.

Then she felt it, the Tar baby had attached itself to her clothing but Jasmine was smart, she wore clothing that was loosely stitched on the side and so as she pulled away from the Tar baby, it took her top clothing and Jasmine continued to run. Jasmine tried running through some mud but her running shoes got stuck. She quickly discarded her shoes and continued to run. She was thankful for all the times when she and Jonathan had ran through Love Hill bare footed and so her soles and heels were as hard as rock.

She knew she was not far from the pit but she could still feel the Tar baby close behind. As she approached the pit, she jumped and skidded to the side. In the Tar baby's haste to catch Jasmine it did not realize that the pit was in front of it and it fell into the bubbling hot tar.

Jasmine watched as the Tar baby melted into the hot tar. She breathes a sigh of relief as she watched her clothes on the surface of the hot tar. At that moment a group of on lookers from the village came to the side of the tar pit. They realized that Jasmine had destroyed the Tar baby. They lifted her onto their shoulders and cheered as they went into the village shouting,

"Jasmine destroyed the Tar baby, Hip, Hip, Hip, and Hooray!"

CHAPTER 9

JASMINE AND JONATHAN AND THE SEARCH FOR THE CREEK OF YOUTH

"Oh daddy, can we please go chapping with you!"

Jasmine pleaded.

"Yes daddy, we can keep up, we won't fall behind and I can carry the crocus bag to put the fish in" Jonathan added.

The two children were trying to convince their father to take them along on his night time fishing expedition. Their father often went chapping in the mangroves for Chad when there was a full moon and a high tide. He would walk through the thick mangroves carrying a search light, a crocus bag to put the fish in and a cutlass to chap the fish as they swam about in the mangroves. The children's father had taken Jonathan on previous occasions and now Jasmine was insisting that he should take her too. Ever since she freed the village of the bad Tar baby she had began to think of herself as invincible.

"Maybe I will take you both another time but it is already after 10pm and you both have school tomorrow. The men who went chapping last night said the shads are there in great abundance and so I should be back in no time," the children's father said.

The children's father was the best fisherman on Love Hill. He was not born there but grew up in a settlement called Lowe Sound. The children of Lowe Sound learnt to swim before they learned to walk and their red hair provided evidence of the amount of time they spent in the sea. They were great divers and craw fishermen and catching bonefish to them was like breathing. When the children's father moved to Love Hill, he was quick to scout out all the fishing grounds on land and in the sea. Every day he woke up and looked at the sky and wondered which fish was biting well that day. He loved fishing so much that he even went at night.

Grandpa Roy also went fishing at night when he was younger. He and the other men in the village would go through the back of Love Hill to fishing grounds that came out in the back of Fresh Creek. They called these fishing grounds "Old House." It was called Old House because of the old plantation house Sound learnt to swim before they learned to walk and their red hair provided evidence of the amount of time they spent in the sea. They were great divers and craw fishermen and catching bonefish to them was like breathing. When the children's father moved to Love Hill, he was quick to scout out all the fishing grounds on land and in the sea. Every day he woke up and looked at the sky and wondered which fish was biting well that day. He loved fishing so much that he even went at night.

When Andros was first populated with free slaves from Africa, they created plantations in the back of Andros but now all of the plantations lay in ruins except for one house that had remained standing. When the fishermen were catching a lot of fish and wanted to stay overnight they would stay at this old house.

There is also a legend that goes with old house. It is believed that somewhere near this fishing ground in the creeks somewhere the water of the sea turn into fresh water.

Under the fresh water in a particular creek is a body of water known as the Creek of Youth. If you swim in this creek and drink from it, you would add from fifty to three hundred years to your life.

Some say this is why the people of Love Hill live to be more than one hundred years old, because they ate the fish that were caught in or had lived in the Creek of Youth.

Grandpa Roy had told Jasmine and Jonathan this story time and time again and they both promised that with their parent's permission they would find the Creek of Youth.

A week later it was summer holidays and Jasmine and Jonathan did not have to go to school. They wanted to go on an adventure and so they went to their father and begged him to tell them what he knew about the Creek of Youth. Their father told them that if they wanted to find the Creek of Youth they would have to find the oldest Andros crab alive and get him to give them directions. The oldest crab alive was about two hundred years old and he lived deep in the coppice of Andros. His home was in the center of a dried up lake. His hole was larger than the largest blue hole and he was surrounded by thousands of land crabs that will not let anyone near the old crab's home. Jasmine and Jonathan were determined to seek out the old crab and discover how to get to the Creek of Youth.

The next day they packed a week's supply of food, an inflatable raft and paddles, a harpoon, spears, walking sticks and a sack of cinder cord. They walked for what seemed like miles in the thick coppice and then as the trees began to thin out they knew they

Their father told them that if they wanted to find the Creek of Youth they would have to find the oldest Andros crab alive and get him to give them directions. The oldest crab alive was about two hundred years old and he lived deep in the coppice of Andros. His home was in the center of a dried up lake. His hole was larger than the largest blue hole and he was surrounded by thousands of land crabs that will not let anyone near the old crab's home. Jasmine and Jonathan were determined to seek out the old crab and discover how to get to the Creek of Youth.

The next day they packed a week's supply of food, an inflatable raft and paddles, a harpoon, spears, walking sticks and a sack of cinder cord. They walked for what seemed like miles in the thick coppice and then as the trees began to thin out they knew they were nearing the Western Coast where most of the crabs hibernated for more than eight months of the year.

After a while, Jasmine and Jonathan came upon the biggest dried up lake they had ever seen and it was filled with thousands of crab holes.

"I guess we need to start walking to the center of the lake to get to the old crab's home," Jonathan said to his sister.

"Well, you're the one who killed the Harbor Master, so I guess I will follow you!" Jasmine exclaimed. "Right!" Jonathan replied sarcastically. "Well, follow me Sis!" Jonathan began walking across the dried up lake followed by Jasmine. They got more confident with every step.

Maybe the crabs were already in hibernation and will not come out of their holes. But after a few more steps, they heard a sound that they were both familiar with.

It was the clicking of crabs but they could tell that there were thousands of them as the clicking got louder and louder and then as if a signal was sent out all of the crabs came out of their holes at the same time. All of the crabs which must have been thousands of them headed toward Jasmine and Jonathan snapping their huge bitters. Jasmine looked at her brother and screamed, "Run come see Jerusalem!"

The crabs were all bigger than the normal size crabs and their biters looked as if they could do a whole lot of damage. Jasmine began to panic and clutched to her brother. Jonathan held her tight and told her not to be afraid.

"Remember our plan Jasmine; climb up on your walking sticks!" Jonathan said.

Jasmine quickly climbed up on her walking sticks. Jonathan threw the sack of cinder cord on his back and climbed up on his walking sticks.

"See the crabs can't get us from up here and the sticks are too narrow, so

They can't climb them up!" Jonathan exclaimed. The brother and sister continued their walk across the dried up lake to the center where they could see a big gaping hole. They were still surrounded by thousands of crabs each trying to clutch onto their walking sticks and hoping that they would fall so they could eat them. At one point Jonathan almost fell as he tried to balance the sack of cinder cord on his back but his sister Jasmine was quick to his rescue, steadying him up.

"Don't worry brother. I've got your back!" Jasmine said with a smile. Jonathan was proud of his little sister.

"I owe you one sis!" Jonathan said gratefully. When they got to the edge of the crab hole, they were shocked.

"Oh goodness! I don't think I want to go down there!" Jasmine exclaimed.

"Well there is no turning back now, just stay close to me," Jonathan comforted his sister.

A mangrove tree grew out the side of the hole and the children used it to climb down. When they got to the bottom, they could hear water running. They turned on their search lights to help them see in the dark. The hole was damp and smelled muddy. They could also smell the scent of crabs. They could see baby crabs running about everywhere and the hole was also infested with snakes. Some of the baby crabs were enjoying their meal of baby snakes. Jasmine looked up and saw a huge foul snake and she screamed. When she screamed, they saw something move in the darkest part of the cave. It began to approach the children. They could see that it had ten legs and two huge biters. It was the old crab and the largest one they had ever seen. The old crab was the size of a fully grown cow. When Jonathan made out the huge crab, he shouted, "Run come see Jerusalem!"

The children were about to run when they heard it speak.

"Why have you come to my hole? Haven't I sent you enough crabs every year to appease your appetite?" said the old crab. "You humans are really unbelievable!"

"We have not come to hurt you," Jonathan replied. "We have come to ask you how to find the Creek of Youth. We have brought you a sack of cinder cord." The children knew that crabs loved cinder cord and this big crab was no exception. When the crab saw the sack of cinder cord, he began to speak again,

"The creek of Youth, yeah I know where it is. In fact I spent the first few years of my life swimming around in it. I guess that is why I have lived so long and grown so big. If I tell you where you can find the Creek of Youth, you must promise never to come here again and never to tell anyone how to find my home," the crab said to the children.

Both of the children agreed to the crab's demand and so he told them how to get to the Creek of Youth. The old crab began to give the children more information.

"You would have to follow the mangrove swamps until they got to the creek. The creek will open up into four main creeks. You must take the creek that is the deepest and follow it up until the water turns from blue to green and then to brown. When the water turns to brown, it will appear that the creek has come to an end but you must continue. The water here is very shallow and in this creek lives a giant barracuda. The barracuda is very vicious and will love to have a human or two for his meal. You must first kill the barracuda because you will not be able to swim in the creek if the creature is still alive," the crab told the adventurous siblings. After some more warnings the children thanked the crab for his assistance and

Take us near, take us far,

Take us to the Creek's sandbar. Jonathan thought his sister's singing was terrible but he did not stop her because he knew she sang when she was bored or afraid. As Jasmine got more confident, she began singing even louder

Waters blue, waters green,

Waters brown, waters plain,

Take us near, take us far,

Take us to the Creek's sandbar.

After a while, they noticed that the water in the creek turned from blue to green and then brown. The brown water was scary looking and Jasmine was frightened that water snakes may be lurking. Before she could finish her thought, she saw two huge red snakes swimming on top of the water. Her mother had climbed out of the crab hole.

Jasmine and Jonathan were amazed to discover that when they returned to the surface the crabs did not attack them. They were able to walk across the dried up lake and the crabs scrambled out of their way to give them safe passage. The children walked until they met the creeks. They inflated their raft and entered the creek. The creek was very deep and

Jonathan reminded his sister to stay in the center of the raft. He did not want her falling overboard. To calm her nerves, Jasmine began to sing,

Waters blue, waters green,

Waters brown, waters plain, always told her that red snakes were doctor snakes. Perhaps these snakes went to swim in the Creek of Youth to prolong their lives as well. As the two snakes swam on top of the water a huge black creature came and cut the two of them in two and then headed toward the raft. It was the giant barracuda. When Jasmine saw the creature, she screamed, 'Look, Jonathan Look, It's the barracuda!"

When Jonathan saw the size of the creature, he shouted, "Run Come See Jerusalem!"

Jonathan reached for his harpoon to spear the barracuda but when he got up to shoot the boat became unbalanced and Jasmine fell overboard. She went under the water kicking and screaming. When she resurfaced, Jonathan reached for his sister with the harpoon.

"Crab a hold of the harpoon and I will pull you in!" Jonathan shouted.

Jasmine struggled to reach for the harpoon. Just as the barracuda was about to bite her, she caught the harpoon and Jonathan pulled her into the boat. Jonathan hugged his sister for a brief moment. If Jasmine got hurt, he would never be able to explain that to his father.

The barracuda circled around and headed back toward the raft. It was determined to have the children for dinner. As he approached the raft Jonathan aimed and fired. The harpoon got the barracuda in the mid-section. The creature was so big and strong that it pulled the raft and the two children behind it as if they were just a little toy. The children screamed as the barracuda took them for the ride of their lives. The barracuda made the mistake in swimming into the shallow creek when it should have swam into the deep creek. The more it swam into the brown shallow creek the thicker the mangroves became. Soon the barracuda swam into a huge mangrove and got entangled. Jonathan then took the opportunity to use all his spears and penetrate the creature. When the creature was dead, Jonathan untangled it from the mangrove and tied the tail of it to the back of the raft to make it easier to pull home.

Jasmine and Jonathan then followed the Old Crab's instruction to find the Creek of Youth. As they neared the place where the crab said it could be found, they noticed that the trees looked greener. The black mangroves were blacker, the red mangroves were redder, and the birds that perched in the trees had radiant glowing feathers. And then they sighted a parrot perched at the top of a mangrove. The parrot was chanting "Creek of Youth, Creek of Youth!". The children followed the parrot's chanting and then they saw it, the water was shining as if it was made out of pure silver. The two children jumped from their raft and into the water. They swam and played and dived below the surface again and again. They also drank as much of it as they could. It tasted delicious. The waters were soft and fresh and clean to the taste.

They could feel every cell in their bodies being revived. It's a pity they could not carry any of the water back with them. The old crab warned them about carrying water back. He said it would kill everything that it came into contact with. The other fish swam about freely in the Creek because they were happy that the barracuda was dead. Jonathan and Jasmine saw species of fish they had never seen before. Some fish had the colors of the rainbow, some had wings like birds and some even had feet to help them walk on the bottom of the creek.

After a while the children reluctantly returned to Love Hill where they shared their adventure with their parents and their fellow villagers. They proudly displayed the huge barracuda as people were fascinated by its size. The barracuda must have been almost two hundred years old to grow to that size. Jasmine and

Jonathan knew they had added at least fifty more years onto their lives but they wondered if anyone would ever notice.

CHAPTER 10

JONATHAN, GRANDPA ROY AND THE ADELINE

Captain Roy was his name and he was the best sailor that the settlement of Love Hill had ever known. He was born the year after a fungus killed the sponge bed and so he was spared the harsh life of spending weeks on the "mud" to make a living. To the villagers he was Captain Roy but to Jonathan he was Grandpa Roy.

Roy, like others had to leave school at the age of twelve and earn his own keep. Roy was drawn to the sea and soon became an excellent sailor. He was able to sail to Nassau from Andros without the aid of navigational instruments and engine powered boats

Roy had spent an entire week mending the sail of the Adeline. The sail was badly torn in the last storm. To mend the sail meant spreading it out in the road and getting all the villagers to come with sail needles to help sew the rips. Jonathan also came with his sail needle to help repair the sail. He could not wait until he and his grandfather set sail on the open seas. When Roy was satisfied with his work, he called his father David to inspect it. David was meticulous when it came to his vessels and he also cared deeply for his oldest son. He would never let him set sail with an unreliable sail.

"Yeah, Roy, this sail is ready. I couldn't do a better job myself!" David said with pride. "You should have smooth sailing tomorrow, the winds should be 15-20 knots, Northeasterly winds. You should reach town in no time."

The next day Roy set sail at the crack of dawn. They passed through the channel that showed the remains of sunken dinghies. He was anxious to reach Nassau because his wife Dollie and Jonathan's sister Jasmine were waiting for them. As Roy entered the ocean he and his first mate, Jonathan spotted the huge shark that patrolled the waters off the Coast of Fresh Creek. The shark was so big that they called him Mr. High Cay after the Cay that could be found off Somerset Creek Beach. Mr. High Cay was so big that when tides were low, he could not enter the Fresh Creek Channel. When Jonathan saw the shark, he looked at his grandpa and both of them shouted at the same time, "Run come see Jerusalem!"

Mr. High Cay swam very close to the Adeline and their pair held their breath. Jonathan could hear his heart pounding in his chest.

The shark was almost twice as long as the vessel itself and it was accompanied with biggest school of grouper the pair had ever seen. The fishermen of Love Hill often told stories of how Mr. High Cay would bring the schools of Nassau grouper in the harbor and take them out. As the groupers passed the pair lowered their nets and before long they could hardly pull up the net with groupers. The fish well of the Adeline was brimming over with grouper and crawfish. Furthermore, the deck was covered with more than two hundred sacks of crabs. Grandpa and grandson knew that they would have a successful trip to Nassau.

Grandpa Roy had always told Jonathan the story about how his father once spotted a treasure chest in Wood Cay Channel but when he went to take it up the water became muddy and he did not see it anymore. Grandpa Roy took Jonathan to the spot in the channel where his grandfather had spotted the treasure chest. He placed the water glass on top of the water and they waited to see if the chest would reveal itself. Just like the story said the chest revealed it and Jonathan could see it clearly through the water glass. "Let's pull it up, Grandpa!" Jonathan yelled with excitement.

"No, we can't touch it!" Grandpa said in a whisper. "It belongs to a ghost pirate, if you move it from there the ghost pirate will follow you."

Now Jonathan did not believe in ghosts and so when Grandpa Roy went below the deck to get his grains to strike some crawfish, Jonathan did the unthinkable. He bent over and took a gaff and pulled up the treasure chest. He then hid it under some empty crates on the deck. Jonathan could not wait to add this to his collection.

All of a sudden it got very dark. It was if night descended with a single second. Grandpa Roy and Jonathan could hardly recognize each other in the dark.

"What is happening Grandpa?" Jonathan asked in a frightened tone.

Before Grandpa Roy could answer they heard a screeching cry

"Prepare to be boarded!" In the dim light Grandpa Roy and Jonathan could make out the sails of another ship alongside the Adeline. They could hear the flag flapping in the wind. They looked up to see two cross bones and a skull on the flag.

Jonathan screamed "Grandpa, it's a ghost ship!" "It's not just a ghost ship. It's a pirate's ghost ship!" replied Grandpa Roy.

"He must be looking for his treasure," Jonathan exclaimed.

"We don't have his treasure!" Grandpa Roy responded.
"Yes, we do Grandpa. I took the treasure when you went below the deck. I didn't believe ghost existed!" Jonathan confessed.

"Boy, you have gotten us in a deep rot!" Grandpa Roy said.

At that very moment a huge pirate boarded the Adeline.

"Prepare to meet your maker!" the one-eyed pirate shouted as he brandished his sword.

Grandpa Roy reached for his grains and threw it at the pirate but it went straight through him. The pirate rushed toward Grandpa who dashed for his cutlass and began to fight the pirate.
"It was not your treasure to begin with!" Grandpa Roy exclaimed.

As Grandpa Roy and the pirate fought, Jonathan raced to get the treasure from its hiding place.

"See your treasure here, take your treasure!" Jonathan shouted to the pirate.

"Too late!" the pirate replied. "I will have my treasure and your head as well!"

Jonathan was afraid. If he had only listened to his Grandpa. He had forgotten that Grandpa told him that whenever you take a dead pirate's treasure you must leave a drop of blood to make sure that they did not haunt you. As Jonathan was still in shock not knowing what to do, he heard Grandpa shout, "Throw the treasure overboard!"

Jonathan dragged the chest to the stern of the vessel and threw it overboard. The pirate jumped overboard after his treasure. As suddenly as the day had become night, the night became day and there was no sign of the ghost ship or the ghostly pirate. Grandpa looked at Jonathan and exclaimed, "Johnny my boy, you must always remember the first rule of the sea, always obey the captain's orders!"

"Yes, Sir!" Jonathan replied, feeling ashamed.

Grandpa Roy and Jonathan continued their journey to Nassau and arrived there before their family could worry about them. Grandpa Roy wasted no time and sold the wood, crabs, crawfish and grouper that he and Jonathan had brought on the Adeline. Then they were able to go shopping and buy bales of flour, rice, grits, tins of lard and salted beef. After a few days Grandpa Roy was ready to return to Andros with his wife and grandchildren. The radio said that a storm was headed for the islands but it was not expected to arrive for a few days. After checking the seas and the sky, Roy was sure that he had enough time to get to Andros before the storm arrived.

"The storm is going to be in the back of us Dollie," Roy assured his wife.

"Whatever you say Roy, you know I trust in God to bring us safely across the ocean," replied Dollie.

Now Dollie was a God fearing woman but she knew Roy was a good sailor, almost as good as her father Yorick. Yorick loved all his children but he named his vessel, the "Dollymae" after her and her sister Mae. Roy always joked that the Dollymae was built too big and was the slowest vessel on the sea. The DollyMae was 28 feet and had a fish well 14 by 14. The Dollymae was shipwrecked and sank off

Blanket Sound after running onto a reef. The accident was not Captain Yorrick's fault as a woman had lit a fire on the beach and while coming into the Sound that night, Yorick mistook the burning beach for a lighthouse beacon and ran upon the reef. Yorick swam safely to shore. The Adeline was only 16 feet but she was sleek and fast and reliable.

They set sail bright and early the next morning. The sea was calm as they left the Prince George Wharf and Roy felt confident that he would reach Andros in no time. After a while the island of New Providence was only a mist and the vessel entered the deep blue waters between Andros and New Providence. Roy knew the water was extremely deep. In fact they called it the tongue of the ocean. Then suddenly the skies got dark and the winds began to blow violently. The waves became bigger and bigger. The vessel rocked from side to side at the mercy of the waves.

"Dollie you and Jasmine go below the deck!" Roy shouted.

Dollie scrambled below the deck with her granddaughter under her arms. She was praying as she went.Captain Roy and the Jonathan began to lower the sails; they knew that the winds were too strong and will tear them to pieces. The strong winds could also break the mast.

"This must be a freak storm!" Captain Roy shouted to Jonathan.

"Maybe it is the storm that they said was approaching the island, they must have given us some wrong information about when it was supposed to arrive!" Jonathan shouted.

"No Soiree! this is a freak storm. This is not going to last very long. As soon as those clouds pass, the wind will break and we will be safe. We must have sailed into a waterspout or what they call a tornado on the seas. Let's just hope that the Adeline can take this beating!"

With those word Roy saw a huge wave approaching, he looked up and shouted,

"Run Come See Jerusalem!"

Roy steered his vessel into the huge wave.

"Maybe we should try and make for a Cay!" shouted Jonathan.

"How will we get Dollie and Jasmine off the boat? The seas are too rough and they would drown!" shouted Roy "I agree!" said Jonathan. The seas are so rough; even I can't swim in this."

"Our best bet is to try and ride out the storm!" Roy shouted back to Jonathan.

'I am going to secure the anchor," shouted Jonathan.

"If that anchor falls over board then we will all be dead!"

Jonathan rushed to secure the anchor. At the very moment they heard a crashing sound as the Adeline hit a rock. The water started to come into the vessel. Roy rushed down below to get buckets to bail out the water.

"What is happening Roy?" Dollie asked anxiously. "The Adeline hit a rock and has sprung a leak; I am going to have to bail out the water!"

"I will help you!" Dollie exclaimed as she jumped to her feet. She instructed Jasmine to bundle up stay below deck.

Captain Roy went back to steering the boat as Dollie and the first mate bailed out buckets and buckets of water.

Meanwhile Captain Roy was busy talking to his vessel,

"Come on baby, you can make it, take Roy home!" Captain Roy then went to his radio and began to make his MAYDAY calls to Nassau, even though he knew they could not really help them because they were too far away for a quick "seek and rescue." "MAYDAY! MAYDAY! MAYDAY!" this is the Adeline and we are requesting assistance. We have sprung a leak; we are located at 77 W Longitude and 24 N Latitude off Fresh Creek, Andros.

After about twenty minutes, but what seemed like hours, it was over. Just like Captain Roy had predicted, the winds stopped and the waves died down but they were still faced with a sinking ship. As fast as they bailed the water out, more came in. Captain Roy went back to his radio

"MAYDAY! MAYDAY! MAYDAY!" He could not let his wife and grandchildren die upon the sea. He taught about his father David and what he would have done. "Steer the vessel Roy, bring her home!" he heard David's voice in his head.

Captain Roy went back to his radio, "MAYDAY! MAYDAY! MAYDAY!" " This is Captain Roy of the Adeline." He felt helpless, only God could save them now. He got no response from Nassau or any nearby vessels but he kept on trying. Then he saw the most frightening thing he had ever seen on the waters; the waters before him seem to bubble and then separate, something huge was surfacing. Could it be the creature that lived in the waters underneath the sea that the Bible had spoken about in Revelation? Captain Roy thought to himself.

While he braced himself for the worst a huge metallic creature rose from below the surface and then the hatch opened up and the captain said,

"I am Captain John Decoda of the SS Barracuda 2; we heard your distress call and we have come to your aid."

Captain Roy could not believe his eyes or his ears. He had always known about the submarine that frequented the waters between Andros and Nassau but he had never come so close to one before.

A group of five navy men exited the submarine, piled onto a small raft and then boarded the Adeline. They assisted Captain Roy and the first mate in stopping the leak. Because the sails on the Adeline were so badly torn the captain of the Submarine instructed his men to tie a rope to the Adeline and he informed Captain Roy. "I am going to give you a tough into safe water"

"Thank you sir. I will appreciate that!"

The submarine pulled the Adeline into safe waters off Fresh Creek Harbor and then disappeared below the surface. Captain Roy was overjoyed, for a moment he thought he would have to leave his vessel. He did not want to be one of those captains who went down with their ships after all; he had a wife, children and grandchildren to think about.

He was grateful that The Adeline did not to join hundreds of vessels that had been shipwrecked in the treacherous waters. As he passed sunken and shipwrecked ships at the mouth of the Fresh Creek harbor, he looked up to the sky and give God thanks. He sure had a story to share with his fellow villagers when he got back to Love Hill. Jonathan could not wait to tell his friends about Mr. High Cay, the ghost ship, the ghostly pirate and the submarine. Dollie testified that it was her prayers and God's intervention that had saved them, Captain Roy, Jonathan and Jasmine were quick to agree.

CHAPTER 11

JONATHAN AND THE HUNT FOR
THE WOODLAND BEAST

"Let's go Jonathan!" Jonathan's father shouted with excitement. "We have to hurry if we are going to catch the beast!"

Jonathan and his father had entered the contest to see who can catch the beast and bring him back alive. Every father with his son on Love Hill had entered the contest but Jonathan was convinced that he and his father were going to win. He believed that his father was the best wild hog hunter on the island of Andros. Wild hogs were actually wild boars that had become indigenous to Andros. These animals were fast and ferocious. They had long tusk that grew out the sides of their faces and if cornered they would attack and kill a human being.

Wild hogs lived in the pine yard and the coppice of Andros and ate crabs, tree roots and whatever wildlife they could find. When food became scarce they would frequent the fields and farms of the natives. The wild hog was an ideal animal to hunt and many hunters used guns and dogs to get their prize.

But once in awhile someone would spot a huge wild hog and everyone would try and bring it back alive.

This huge wild hog was called the beast because of its abnormal size. It was considered to be special therefore one could not use dogs or guns while hunting it. In fact, you were expected to tame the wild beast and bring it home walking in front of you or behind you. If the beast was captured, it was believed to bring good luck to the village and the entire village would enjoy a good wild hog hunting season. The prize for capturing the beast was being named father and son of the year and the pair got to lead every hunting party and would also get the largest share of all the catch. Your name would also be engraved in the town hall and a picture of father and son would be mounted.

Jonathan and his father went out that day in search of the beast. They like all the other hunters did not find the beast. Nevertheless, they were able to capture two ordinary wild hogs which they grilled over an open fire and everyone in the village was treated to a free meal.

"No one can catch that beast. He is just to smart. Only one beast has been caught in more than fifty years, we might as well forget this contest!" Jonathan's father said to the other hunters as they ate their fill of wild hogs.

"No daddy, we must keep looking!" Jonathan said sadly.

"Your father is right!" said Poke, the oldest man in the settlement.

Poke must have been one hundred and fifteen years old and he knew everything that happened on Love Hill. In fact, he was like the town's librarian, historian and oracle. People took his advice seriously as he was never wrong about anything. He had what the old people called mothers' wit and wisdom.

"To find that old beast, you must first find the night owl that use to perch above the old coconut tree by the water well. If you can convince the old owl to tell you where to find the beast, he may even tell you how to tame it as well!" Poke told the villagers.

Now everyone knew that the old owl had not been spotted there in more than ten years and everyone believed that the old owl had finally died.

Jonathan was determined for him and his father to win this contest and so he went to an old friend who he believed could help him. Jonathan went into the pine forest the next day in search of the Chickcharnie.

He had kept the Chickcharnie's secret and since he always showed the funny looking bird man the greatest respect they had remained good friends over the years. When Jonathan arrived at the two pine trees that held the new nest of his friend he called to him and the Chickcharnie swooped down and carried Jonathan into his nest.

"What can I do for you my little friend?" asked the Chickcharnie.

"I would like for you to tell me where I can find the old owl," Jonathan replied.

"Why do you want to find the old owl?" enquired the Chickcharnie.

"Because the beast has been sighted and my father and I would like to capture him, tame him and win the prize. I believe you can tell me where I can find the old owl," Jonathan told his friend the Chickcharnie.

"I will tell you where you can find the old owl but you must promise me that you will not try to capture it or hurt it as the old owl is my cousin," responded the chickcharnie. Jonathan agreed.

The Chickcharnie told Jonathan that if he wanted to find the Old owl he would have to travel to the southern point of the district known as Behring Point. At the end of the point he would come upon a sisal field with fully grown sisal plants. The owl lives in this field for protection from humans as the field is difficult to walk through without being stuck. If one tries to cut the sisal, the juice from the sisal will cause you to itch unbearably. In the centre of the sisal field grows the tallest sisal tree and there you will find the old owl perched. You must greet the owl with respect and ask for his assistance. Jonathan thanked his friend, the Chickcharnie, and raced home to share the information with his father.

The next day Jonathan and his father headed for Behring Point. They had to pass through the settlements of Small Hope, Calabash Bay, Fresh Creek, Bowen Sound, Cargil Creek and finally Behring Point. At the end of the settlement they came upon the thick Sisal plantation and since they knew they could not use a cutlass or machete to cut their way through, they had to hold each sisal plant as they went, moving them out of their way, dodging under and leaping over. This method took a long time but they avoided being stuck and were itch free. When they got to the centre of the field, they looked up and saw the old owl and they greeted him respectfully.

"Wise old owls, wiser than all birds, tell us what you know!" Jonathan's father asked. The owl did not respond and so Jonathan tried. "Wise old owls, wiser than all birds, tell us what you know!" Jonathan asked.

The old owl did not respond and so Jonathan and his father tried together.

"Wise old owls, wiser than all birds, tell us what you know!"

"Now that's the way you ought to ask!" replied the old owl. "Teamwork will help you to defeat any obstacle. Now what do you want to know?" replied the owl.

"We would like to know where we can find the woodland beast and how to tame it?" Jonathan's father replied.

"Because you did not destroy my sisal trees which provide me with a safe haven from animals and people, I will tell you what you want to know. The woodland beast can be found living in a strong bar field on the west side of the island. The pair thanked the wise old owl for his help and started their long journey home.

Jonathan and his father decided to get plenty of rest that night before they set out to search for the woodland beast the next day.

They knew they had to be fit, as they had to run fast and long to be able to exhaust the beast. They knew BLC was an old deserted village in the interior of Andros that was left by the Bahamas Lumber Company which once cut down pine trees for export. It was a good spot to hunt for wild hogs because of the abundance of berries and good water supply. When Jonathan and his father arrived at BLC, they climbed up a tree to see if they would spot the beast. After a while the beast came to the lake to drink. The beast was huge. It was almost the size of a small car and must have weighed about two tons. It was covered with brownish, reddish hair and four tusks grew out the side of its face. The tusks were as long as foot long rulers. The beast was a frightening sight and when the pair saw it they both screamed at the same time, "Run come see Jerusalem!"

They waited until the beast had drunk its fill in the hopes that the water would weigh him down and make him easier to catch and then they bounced on him. But the beast was fast and strong and was able to throw both Jonathan and his father flying into the air.

They got up and pursued the beast that ran through the forest, grunting and clearing everything in its path. For a moment it got stuck in the mud and the pair thought they had him but the beast was so agile and so strong that he escaped them and the mud.

As Jonathan and his father emerged from the mud, one could not tell who the beast was.

They ran behind the beast for what seemed like hours through the pine forest and finally the beast showed signs of exhaustion.

Jonathan used this opportunity to throw a rope around the beast head and then his father quickly tied the rope to a tree. The pair then continued to run behind the beast as he circled the tree over and over again. Finally, Jonathan's father was able to grab a hold of the beast's hind legs but the beast continued to run around the tree, dragging Jonathan's father behind him. But Jonathan's father was determined and would not let go. Jonathan and his father then took turns holding the beast hind legs until the beast was finally broken and he began to walk around the tree. When the pair was certain that the beast was tamed they loaded him on the back of the truck and headed for Love Hill.

Before they entered the settlement, they untied the beast, took it by the hind legs and led him into the settlement. Everyone came out shouting and cheering, "They have caught the beast and they have tamed it as well!"

Jasmine raced home to tell her mother,

"Daddy and Jonathan have caught the beast and they have tamed it as well!"

Jasmine's mother shouted,

"My boys have caught the beast and they have tamed it as well!"

CHAPTER 12

JONATHAN AND JASMINE AND THE SECRET OF THE TWO KEYS

"Sweet potato, Sweet potato, Sweet Potato Pie

I love to eat my sweet potato pie,

Sweet potato, sweet potato, sweet potato pie

My mom is baking sweet potato pie."

Jasmine sat on the porch singing this tone to herself over and over again. Her mother had dug some sweet potato out of the garden and was baking some sweet potato pie. Jasmine could not wait for the pie to done as she loved to eat sweet potato pie.

Jonathan was becoming annoyed with his sister's singing and so he said "Greedy girl singing for her supper, why don't you come and help me search through my treasure chest!"

"Sweet potato, sweet potato, sweet potato pie,
I love to eat my sweet potato pie,

Sweet potato, sweet potato, sweet potato pie

My mom is baking sweet potato pie." Jasmine sang even louder.

"If you help me search my treasure chest, I will give you my share of sweet potato pie," Jonathan said to his sister.

"Do you promise?" Jasmine asked excitedly.

"You have my word!" Jonathan replied.

So Jasmine stopped singing and went to help her brother search through his treasure chest.

After playing with the many gold and silver coins, pearls and gold plates, the children came across two huge keys on a string. Somehow they had never noticed the keys before and now they wondered what door or doors the keys would unlock. The keys each had a strange symbol on them which the children did not recognize. After a long time of guessing what the keys were for they went to their mother and asked her.

The children's mother looked at the keys and after a while said that one of the keys has a symbol that looked like an "L" and the other had a symbol that looked like an "H". Since their mother could not help them any further, they went to their father but he was not able to help them either. So they went to Grandpa Roy. As soon as Grandpa Roy saw the keys he shouted aloud Well, Run come see Jerusalem!" I thought that the legend of the two keys was a fake. There must be some truth to that old story!" Grandpa Roy exclaimed.

"What story?" the children shouted together.

So Grandpa Roy told them of the story of the two keys. "It is believed that the old lighthouse at fresh Creek Harbor had a hidden door and behind that hidden door is information about a place that once existed. However, no one has ever found the hidden door and people stopped searching the lighthouse almost one hundred years ago because it is believed to be haunted," Grandpa told the children.

"Haunted!" the children screamed at the same time. Yes, it is believed that a female ghost haunts the old lighthouse and she scares off anyone who tries to enter. Maybe she is protecting the secret of the two keys," Grandpa Roy whispered to the children. "How did the ghost come to live in the light house?" Jonathan asked.

"I don't know," Grandpa replied. "Maybe you should go and ask Poke, he knows everything."

So the children went and asked Poke. Poke was happy to share what he knew with the children.

As Poke began, he leaned toward the children, "Some people believe that she is the ghost of a woman who died in a ship wreck off Fresh Creek. Others believe that she is the ghost of a woman buried in the cemetery near to the light house.

When Andros was first settled by free Africans in the 1800s, people did not have machines to dig graves in the solid ground and so all of the cemeteries were located on the beach. It was easy to dig graves in the sand and so everyone was buried on the beach just above the high tide mark. They stopped burying people on the beach after the bodies kept coming out of their coffins and above the surface during heavy storms and hurricanes. Maybe this ghost was one of those persons who came out of her coffin and then took a new home in the light house. However, some people believe that she could also be the ghost of a woman who died on the Bitoria in 1930.

The people who perished on the Bitoria were never given a proper burial and so their spirits wander up and down the beach. For many years after the sinking of the Bitoria, the people who lived in the settlements of Fresh Creek and Love Hill said that on the anniversary of the sinking of the schooner, they could hear the ghosts of those who perished walking and screaming up and down the beach as they headed for Blanket Sound.

Some of the ghosts would be screaming,

"Come for me!", "somebody, come for me!"

Many people were afraid to walk the beaches during the month of February and especially at night!" Poke told the children.

"Ghosts are not real Mr. Poke!" Jasmine said. "That's right Mr. Poke, my mummy said the dead don't have any power, therefore, ghosts do not exist!" Jonathan supported his sister.

"Well children, if you don't believe in ghosts, then there is no more I can say to you. But if you ever come upon one remember to repeat the 23rd Psalms and that will keep you safe," Poke told the siblings. The children agreed that Mr. Poke knew a lot, but one thing he did not know was how to tell when something was real and when something was not. The siblings had a good laugh, "Ghosts, Ha! Ha! Ha!".

The children could not wait to return home to devise a plan to search the old lighthouse and discover the secret of the two keys. After they had informed their mother that they were going on an adventure they headed for the old lighthouse. Their new bikes that they got for Christmas would get them to Andros Town in no time.

They knew the old lighthouse was deserted and the road to it had grown up. They also knew that trees and vines covered the old building. They were careful to wear long sleeved clothing, tennis shoes and take with them searchlights and a cutlass to chap away the over growth of trees. The children were not afraid of ghosts, In fact they were hoping to see one and so

Jasmine took her camera along to take a picture. When the children got to the beach, they parked their bikes and began to walk. As they walked, they looked down, careful of every step they took, wondering whether they were walking on any graves.

When they got to the tract road that led to the old lighthouse they had to use the cutlass to chap away the bushes. As they were chapping, they accidentally chapped a wasp's nest and had to run as fast as they could but not before each of them had gotten some very nasty stings about the face. Their faces were swollen by the time they reached the old lighthouse. "Don't worry Jasmine if there is a ghost and she sees your face, I think she will run away!" Jonathan teased his sister.

Yes, and if she sees your face, I know she will come to life!" Jasmine retaliated.

The two children laughed at each other and then they remembered that they should search the old lighthouse before it got dark. Just as they were both about to enter the lighthouse, Jasmine spotted two old cannons, pointing in their direction she said to Jonathan, "Can you take a picture of me standing near the old cannons?"

Jonathan replied, "Oh, but of course sis"

She stood in front of the old cannon as Jonathan snapped a shot.

"What do you think the first key is for?" Jonathan asked his sister.

"Maybe, it opens the door to the lighthouse," Jasmine replied.

So Jonathan tried the key in the huge door and to the children's amazement the key clicked. Then both of them pushed against the door to open it. When they were finally inside, they could tell that the lighthouse had not been opened for almost a century. It was dark, damp and smelled musty.

The children ascended the wooden staircase to the top of the lighthouse and when they got there they saw a breath taking view of Fresh Creek Harbor. It was simply beautiful.

The turquoise water in the channel was clear and they could see the white sand on the sea bottom.

The blue waters joined the green waters where the shallow sea met the ocean and the sight of it was simply divine.

The wave that breaks over the reef forming white foam on the water was fascinating and seemed to be calling the ships as they passed. Now the children understood why the ghost would want to live in the lighthouse.

"Let's look for another door!" Jonathan shouted.

"Yes, let's look!" Jasmine replied.

So the children went back down stairs and began searching for another door. There was no other door in sight. Then Jasmine began to feel the walls and noticed that most of the walls felt cold but there was an area where the wall felt warm. Jonathan began to feel the warm wall as well and then discovered that there was a hole in the wall, a hole that was the shape of a key hole. Jonathan used the second key and heard a click. Then the children had to use all the strength they had to push the door open as it was made of stone.

When the door was opened, they could not see a thing. They turned on their searchlights and descended some cement steps that went below the lighthouse. When they got to the bottom of the step, they could make out a chest in the corner of the tiny room. They walked over to it.

"Should we open it?" Jonathan asked his sister. "Why not, we have come this far," Jasmine said to her brother.

And so the two children opened the chest and the only thing they saw was a tattered old map.

"What does the map say?" Jasmine asked her brother. "It says, the City of Atlantis, located of Andros Island in the Bahamas," Jonathan replied.

"Do you think the map is real?" Jasmine asked. "I don't know, but I've never heard of any old city called Atlantis either, it must not be important," Jonathan said disappointedly.

At that same moment, the children heard a screeching sound. It was almost like a wailing. They rushed up to the top of the stairs to see a ghostly figure of a woman dressed in white coming down from the top of the stairs. It was the ghost that the children did not believe existed. Jasmine shouted to Jonathan and pointed to the ghost at the same time. Jonathan shouted,

"Well, I'll be, Grandpa Roy and Poke were right, Run come see Jerusalem!"

The ghost headed toward the children with her hands outstretched. Her feet were not touching the ground figure; she had pale, white skin, long silver hair, a very old and wrinkled face which was also twisted. She wore a long suit of white which looked like a burial shroud. The ghost's intention was to scare the children and if they were much older they might have suffered a heart attack.

The children knew that she was not the ghost of a slave or a descendant of a slave. Nor could she be the ghost of anyone who perished on the Bitoria because all of the passengers were black. She must be the ghost of a white plantation owner or someone who perished in a shipwreck off the East Coast of Andros.

The ghost headed toward the door as if to prevent the children's escaped. The big heavy door began to close by itself, making a screeching sound.

The wind started to blow from somewhere and they and she waded in the air. She was a horrific looking could also hear the angry waves of the sea as they crash against the rocks. The children wished Poke was there and then they remembered what he said. They began to repeat the 23 Psalm, "The Lord is my Shepherd and I shall not want...." before the children could finish the Psalm, the ghost retreated up the stairs and the door began to open again.

"Take a picture!" Jonathan shouted to Jasmine.

"You take a picture, I am out of here!" Jasmine yelled. The two children raced out of the old lighthouse leaving behind the map and the camera and the cutlass and their searchlights.

As they rode their bikes home, they began to promise each other not to tell a single soul how they were chased away by a ghost. They wondered if they should go back for their possessions and the map. "We could do that on another adventure," Jonathan said to his baby sister.

Jasmine was quick to agree.

When they returned home their mother was waiting with the sweet potato pie but both of the children were quick to say,

"No thank you!" They had both lost their appetite and only wanted to go to bed.

"Well, how was your adventure?" their mother asked. The children looked at each other but they could not utter a word.

CHAPTER 13

JASMINE AND JONATHAN AND THE PRICKLE PATCH

"Ouch!", "Ouch!", "Ouch!" were the cries of everyone in the little settlement of Love Hill. It was Mid-December and the winds were blowing ferociously, but this year it was different. The winds brought hundreds of thousands of prickles into the settlement. There was prickle on all the clothes, prickle on the animals, prickle on the houses, cars, porches, plants and trees. No one could be outside because they would be covered in prickles in less than a minute.

Jonathan and Jasmine raced home from school, but this time they were trying to get into the house as quickly as they could. The prickles were all over them and when they got inside, they had the tedious task of picking them off their clothing. As they picked the prickles away, they got stuck in their fingers and so you could hear them saying, "Ouch!, Ouch!, Ouch!" "How long is the wind going to keep blowing?" Jasmine asked her mother.

"The winds should keep blowing up until the end of February," her mother replied.

"Does that mean that we have to endure the prickles until then?" Jasmine asked.

"Yes Jasmine, unless someone goes to destroy that old Prickle patch." There is a huge mother prickle patch that is making all of these prickles. As long as the wind is blowing and the mother prickle patch is making prickles then I am afraid we will have to endure these terrible conditions," Jasmine's mother replied.

Jonathan and Jasmine knew that their mother was very sad. The prickle patch had destroyed her beautiful garden and killed all of her plants and vegetables. To make matters worse she was forced to stay inside and she preferred to be outdoors. The children felt sad for their mother. They knew that they had to destroy the prickle patch so their mother could start smiling again. That night they devised a plan. Before the break of dawn the next day, the children were on their way to find the prickle patch and destroy it.

They knew they could find the prickle patch by looking at the direction from which most of the prickles were blowing from. They determined that to be a Northeasterly direction and so they headed into the prickles.

They wore long sleeved clothing to protect their skin and goggles to protect their eyes. They wore gloves to protect their hands and caps to protect their heads. Not a single inch of their bodies were left uncovered. They even were cloth masks on their faces to protect their faces and slits were made in the masks to allow room for breathing. They did not cut slits for talking and spoke through the cloth; this was to prevent prickles from flying into their mouths when they spoke.

After they had walked for many miles, they were exhausted. They had to push hard against the wind and this tired them out even more. At lunch time they stopped to get something to eat. They tried to eat their sandwiches, but before they could get them under their masks and into their mouths, the sandwiches were filled with prickles. Soon they gave up trying to eat and chose to drink some water from their water jugs.

The children continued their walk until they came upon the prickle patch field. They could feel the prickles in the wind getting thicker and thicker and they could feel more prickles on the ground. Before long they were in the prickle patch field. As they walked toward the gigantic hole that held the mother prickle patch they began to bog in prickle. Soon prickles caught them to their knees.

When they got to the hole, they saw the most terrifying sight. A mother prickle patch tree was shooting out thousands of prickles at a time and the wind was picking them up and blowing them over the land. Jasmine and Jonathan knew that the only way to destroy the prickle patch would be to set it afire but they had to be careful not to get caught in the flames. Jonathan instructed Jasmine to take a rope and tie it to the far end of the field. He then took the other end and climbed down into the prickle patch hole and attached it to the plant. They both planned to light the far end of the rope and let the fire lead itself to the prickle patch hole. In the meantime they would be making their escape by running as fast as they could, out of the prickle patch field. Jonathan had already scouted the nearby surroundings and he had spotted a blue hole. He and Jasmine would run as fast as they could to the blue hole and jump into it. They planned to out run the fire and if the fire gets as far as the blue hole, it should pass over them.

"We should be safe in the blue hole, fire can't burn on water," Jonathan said to his sister.

"I hope it does not burn long, remember we can't swim forever," Jasmine replied.

To give herself courage, Jasmine began singing to herself,

Prickle patch, Prickle patch, bad old prickle patch,

We must destroy the bad old prickle patch,

Prickle patch, prickle patch, bad old prickle patch

Today, you meet your match, bad old prickle patch.

"Are you ready Sis?" Jonathan asked.

"Ready as I'll ever be!" Jasmine replied.

"Well, let's do it!" Jonathan shouted.

The two children went to the edge of the field and was about to light the rope when they saw a terrifying figure coming towards them. Out of the hole rose a huge prickle patch Mummy. The Mummy was made out of prickles and was about six feet tall. Seeing the prickle patch mummy made Jasmine remember the Tar baby and she began to scream. The children did not plan on fighting a Prickle Patch Mummy and they were both left speechless.

The Prickle Patch Mummy headed toward the children spraying prickles on its approach. Soon the two children were covered in prickles. The prickles were sharp and began to penetrate the children's clothing and hurt them.

"We must make a run for it Sis!" Jonathan screamed to his sister.

As the children ran, the Prickle Patch Mummy pursued them. Jonathan urged his sister to continue running and he returned to light the rope. Jonathan lit the rope and the children watched as the fire traveled along the rope toward the prickle patch hole. When the fire got to the hole, there was a loud sound, like a big explosion as the mother prickle patch plant exploded. The children knew that they had to start running. Soon the entire field was engulfed in flame and so was the Prickle Patch Mummy. They ran as fast as they could through the forest, toward the blue hole. They could feel the heat of the fire behind them and they could hear the sound of brushes and trees burning.

They could smell the scent of burning brush and they could see smoke in the air. Jonathan ran behind Jasmine even thought he was faster than she was. He did not want to leave her behind. As she started to slow down, he shouted to his sister,

"Run like the wind Jasmine, run like the wind!" The children reached to the blue hole before the fire and they dived into it. As they jumped into the air, they shouted at the top of their voices,

"Run come see Jerusalem!"

As they landed in the cool waters below, they looked up to see balls of smoke and fire pass over the blue hole. They had made it just in time. It was a stunning picture to look up and see fire in a circle all around them, but they were safe in the cool blue waters. They shouted for joy and give each other high fives. "We did it!" Jonathan exclaimed.

"Yes we did," Jasmine replied as she began to sing "We're fast, we're quick, we're dangerous, we're fast, we're quick, and we're dangerous!"

Jonathan soon got a hang of the tone and joined his sister.

After the children got tired wading, floating and diving in the water, they climbed up on a shelf inside the blue hole and started to relax. They were then faced with a new problem. The animals that had out ran the fire also sought refuge in the blue hole. Soon the blue hole was filled with lizards, snakes, iguanas and wild life of all kinds. However, the animals were so afraid and so happy to be safe from the fire that none of them bothered the children or each other. Jasmine and Jonathan waited until they thought it was safe and they climbed out of the blue hole. The wind was still blowing but the field was smooth and as level as a football field and there was not a single prickle in sight.

Jasmine and Jonathan jumped for joy as they sang their little song

We're fast, we're quick, we're dangerous, we're fast, we're quick, and we're dangerous!"

Now it was time to go home but the children were faced with a new problem. They did not know which way to go. They had burned down all the trees that stood as landmarks and there was no sight of a tract or foot path. The sky was still filled with smoke and many dark clouds had moved in and as a result they could not tell where the sun was to indicate which direction they should take. All of the tall trees were burnt in the fire and so they could not climb a tree to see where they should go. Jasmine became frightened and began to cry. She could not bear the thought of being lost. She was lost once before with her class and it took her a very long time to get over that.

"Don't cry, Jasmine," Jonathan said to his baby sister.

"I'll figure something out, I always do".

Jonathan sat down to think. As Jonathan sat down to think, he remembered that when they were coming in search of the prickle patch that they were facing the wind. To return home they had should have the wind at their backs.

Jonathan pulled his sister to her feet and said, "Follow me, I know the way." Jonathan sure did. In no time they were back home at their house in Love Hill. They had walked faster as the wind was at their back and pushed them along. They met everyone out in their yards, happy and smiling. There were no prickles in sight as the wind had blown them away. When the children's mother saw them, she ran and hugged and kissed her children.

"I knew you could do it!" she said to her children.

"We did it for you, mummy!" the children responded.

CHAPTER 14

JASMINE AND JONATHAN AND AN AFTERNOON WITH GRANDPA ROY

"Clash, clash, clash!" went the swords as Jasmine and Jonathan played pirates with the swords out of Jonathan's collection. Jonathan was pretending to be Blackbeard the pirate and Jasmine was pretending to Anne Boney, the pirate. They were dressed in pirate's clothes and looked as dreadful as the pirates. The children's mother came into the room and when she saw her two children she screamed.

At first she taught they were real pirates and then she recognized them as her children. Filled with embarrassment and fear for her children playing with real swords, she insisted that they stop the game at once and get a book to read. The children did not want to read the same old boring stories so they convinced their mother to let them go and spend the afternoon with Grandpa Roy.

The children loved spending time with Grandpa Roy as he always told them fascinating stories about his youth which he referred to as the "good old days." The things that their Grandpa experienced were so horrific that they referred to them as the "bad old days."

The children raced each other down the hill toward their grandpa's house. When they arrived at the house, they met their grandpa feeding the goats.

They hurried to help him as they also loved feeding the goats. The goats were enjoying a delicious meal of jumbay and cinder cord. Jasmine and Jonathan had named all the goats and they called each one by name.

Afterwards, they followed Grandpa under the fig tree where he would tell those stories. Grandpa had also chapped opened some tried coconuts and the children helped themselves in putting sugar on the inside of the coconuts and using a spoon to rake the sugar and coconut. It was a sweet coconut treat. "Grandpa, tell us the story about your school days and how you had to walk to school!" Jonathan said. "Well, children, in those days, we did not have buses to take us to school and so we had to walk all the way from Love Hill to Calabash Bay, every day and back again. That would be about fourteen miles every day.

The bad thing was that the children of Love Hill were always late to school because we had to get up early in the morning and walk to Brazeletto Hill to cut wood. After we had cut the wood, we would have to walk about ten miles with the wood on our heads and then we would have to walk out to sea for the tide to float the wood off our head.

If we tried to throw the wood down, it would break our necks. Towing the wood on the top of our heads made the top of our heads flat. That is why most men who are from Love Hill have flat top heads and bald plates.

After we had gotten the wood then we would have to try and rush off to school with our breakfast, which was also lunch. Our breakfast/ lunch consisted of a huge piece of potato bread which we placed in our pockets.

That potato bread was so hard and heavy that a few bites of that were enough to keep us full all day. Sometimes it was burnt at the bottom because it was baked outside in a rock oven or in a cast iron pot over an open fire. The boys of Love Hill were always late in getting to school. We always tried to get to school early but when we got to the settlement of Small Hope, we had to run and take to the beach because the bad dogs would not let us pass. When we finally got to school, the children of Calabash Bay and Fresh Creek teased us "Lazy John when the sun was rising, turn thy face from the rising sun," a popular British poem that the children recited at that time.

That made me remembers what the white plantation owners use to sing to my aunty and others on the Prince Wharf Dock. They sang, Lazy bum sitting in the sun, can't get a day's work done.

Furthermore, the principal would be waiting there, ready to cane us for being late," Grandpa told the children. School days were hard days for us Love Hill boys but still we learnt our lesson.

"Did you like going to school, Grandpa?" Jasmine asked.

"Yeah, I liked school because I was smart. We had to write on slate and memorize everything before it was erased. We did not have pencils and notebooks as you have today.

Unfortunately, we had to leave school at the age of twelve. We had to go and earn a living cutting wood or craw fishing. We Andros boys always had it hard. Many of others had to leave the island to find work," Grandpa Roy said sadly. It was worst for Daddy and Uncle those who had to go sponging on Mud. They were gone for six weeks at a time and when they returned home they brought very little money and flour and grits laden with weevils. They were paid in Kind and this was known as the Trucking System. Uncle was so tired of slaving on the Mud that he said that God had sent the fungus to destroy the sponge beds because of the injustice the Andros men were suffering.

"Did you ever have to leave Andros to look for work, Grandpa?" Jonathan asked.

"Yeah boy, I went to Chub Cay and worked there when they built the resorts. I went to Grand Bahama and worked there when they started the city of Freeport and I worked on the first Paradise Island Bridge. Boy, that Paradise island bridge job was an experience. I remembered going down under the water to pour the cement pillars as I was an underwater carpenter and I had to use 70lb weights to keep me down. While I was under there, a huge shark came straight toward me. This was a humongous shark and they called him the Harbor Master because he patrolled the harbor between the British Colonial Hotel and the bridge. I signal for the men above to pull me up as they could see me through the water glass. When they pulled me up, I swore never to go back down there again," Grandpa said.

The children looked at each other and began to laugh. They could imagine the look on their Grandpa's face as the shark approached him. Now they know why he is so afraid of sharks.

"What did you say when you saw the shark?
Grandpa?" asked Jasmine.
"Pretty gal, you know what I said, Run come see Jerusalem!" Grandpa exclaimed.

"What about the time when you ended up in the cemetery?" Jasmine asked.

"Oh, yeah, the cemetery," Grandpa Roy responded. "Yes, I had been to the bar in Calabash and was having a very good time. It was far after midnight when I decided to go home. I was driving my first truck, an old T- model Ford and as I ascended the hill to Love Hill, I saw a ghostly figure in the road and I swayed to avoid hitting the ghost and my truck ended up in the cemetery on top of a tombstone. I tried to open the door but something told me that I should not get out of the truck. As I look around, I could see the spirits of the dead people coming out of their graves and coming out of the cemetery. My house was not far from the cemetery and so I began to scream for my mother. Mother! , Mother! , Mother! , I screamed. My father heard me screaming and said, that's Roy in the cemetery, leave him alone Nicey, He bloody well had rights to come home before midnight. My mother said No, David, I have to go and get my child. Now, my mother had only one leg but she got on her crate which she used to help her move about and dragged over the rocks to the cemetery to help me. If my mother had not come and rescue me, those spirits were going to carry me. Nevertheless, I never stayed out late again and was always home in the house before midnight."

"Grandpa, how do you know what you saw were real spirits and not the spirits you were drinking?" Jonathan asked.

"Well, son I will never know, but I will tell you one thing; you should never drink and drive!" Grandpa replied.

"Why did the old people in your days hang bottles in the tree, Grandpa?" Jonathan asked.

"Well, in those days' things were tough and people did not have much. A person who had fruit trees like ginep, sugar apples, dilly and sour oranges in his or her yard were considered important. Since they did not want anyone to steal their fruit, they would go in the grave yard, take some grave yard dirt and put into the bottles and then hang the bottles in the trees where everyone could see. If you stole off the tree, you would have a very bad pain in the stomach or some people believed that you would even die?" Grandpa Roy said.

"Did anyone ever die of eating of the tree without asking?" Jasmine asked.

"Not that I know off, I think it was a way to make sure that thieves did not get your scarce fruits," Grandpa said with a laugh. "In fact, in those days it was an offence to steal people's coconuts and if you did the Commissioner could sentence you to one year in jail for each coconut."

"Tell us about the time when you and your cousin went to the Sunshine Twin in Nassau?" Jonathan asked eagerly.

"Yeah, my cousin and I were young at that time and we had collected our Friday paycheck and when we had taken out our parent's share to send to Andros, we decided to treat ourselves to a movie. It was the first time I had gone to the show and I was looking good and shining. We were watching a war movie and when the plane flew over, I thought the plane was coming toward me so I shouted Holy Moses, dodge, George dodge. I then jumped out of my seat and dodged as low as I could. Everyone in the movie show laughed at me.

After the movie we met to fine ladies and they asked us to give them a ride home. We agreed because the girls were nice looking and we were true gentlemen. But as we were passing the cemetery, they said, you'll can let us off here. My cousin and I looked at them and laughed and then we said but that's the cemetery. One of the girls said, we know, we have to get home before two o'clock and then they disappeared out of the car. When we looked over at the cemetery, we saw the two girls going through the gate. My cousin and I raced home and we never gave strange girls a ride again," Grandpa Roy whispered to the children.

"Was that really true?" Jasmine asked.

"As true as the sea is the color blue!" Grandpa replied. "Grandpa, tell us about the wedding reception you attended when you were a teenager," Jasmine said. "Well, pretty gal, you know in those days a wedding reception in a small village was a big thing. Everyone dressed up in their finest or Sunday go to church clothes, put on hats and wigs and attended the reception. It was our opportunity to show off our clothes as well as our dances. We could dance dances like smash the potato and smash the cockroach. At one wedding reception, Lil thing got drunk because someone mixed his drink and he became unruly and wanted to beat up everyone. The elders in the village called for the biggest and strongest men to calm him down but Lil thing beat them up, one by one. Lil Thing was small and short but he was very strong. First they called the constable but Lil Thing piked him up and dashed him to the ground, he went crying home to his wife. Then they called Bulla. Bulla was about 6feet 8 inches and weighted about three hundred and fifty pounds but Lil thing grabbed Bulla and body slammed him. Bulla went home to his wife and was sick in bed for weeks after that. The then called Heads. Heads was accustomed to towing two to three hundred pound Mahogany and Madeira wood on his head. Heads grabbed for Lil Thing but Lil Thing wheeled him around and flung him to the ground.

Heads was smart and quickly made his escape. They then called for Boogaloo. Boogaloo was a professional boxer and could take down any man. Boogaloo got a few boxes on Lil Thing but they did not affect him at alone. However, when Lil Thing returned the boxes on Boogaloo, he knocked Boogaloo out cold. The ladies in the settlement dragged Boogaloo home. Finally they called for my father and my uncle. The pair attacked Lil Thing at the same time. While my uncle kicked him below the belt, my daddy cow belled him from behind and that brought Lil Thing to his knees. They quickly tied Lil Thing up until the booze wore off and he came to his normal senses" Grandpa said with a laugh.

"What is the moral of that story, Grandpa?" asked Jonathan.

"The moral of that story is a drunken man is a dangerous man, therefore you should watch what you drink!" Grandpa replied.

"Tell us some more stories about your young days Grandpa!" Jasmine begged.

"No, now it is time for you children to be heading home, it's getting late and your mother will become worried," Grandpa Roy said to the children. "On your way, be careful not to talk to strangers and if you spot any Jack Ma Lanterns, Run like the wind."

With these words in their heads, the two children raced home as fast as they could, never looking backwards or sideways but straight ahead. They made it home in record time.

THE ADVENTURES OF JONATHAN AND JASMINE ON ANDROS ISLAND

COMPREHENSION QUESTIONS AND EXPRESS YOURSELF (COMPOSITION PRACTICE)

JONATHAN: THE CHICKCHARNIE, THE MERMAID AND THE HARBOR MASTER

1. Who is the main character in the story?
2. Where does the story take place?
3. What did Jonathan do when he got bored?
4. Describe a Chickcharnie?
5. What is a Mermaid's appearance?
6. What is a Harbor Master?
7. According to the story, what would happen if you laugh at a Chickcharnie?
8. Why did the Chickcharnie give Jonathan a pot of gold?
9. Where did Jonathan meet the Mermaid?
10. What is promised to you, if you keep the Mermaid's secret?
11. How did the Chickcharnie help Jonathan?
12. Why did the Mermaid help Jonathan escape from the Harbor Master?
13. How did Jonathan kill the Harbor Master?
14. Suggest another title for this story.
15. Create a list of three things that are fact in the story and three things that are fiction in the story.

EXPRESS YOURSELF

Imagine you are Jonathan, write a short story about how you used the treasure you got from the Chickcharnie and the Mermaid.

JONATHAN AND THE SEARCH FOR THE ARAWAK VILLAGE

1. Who is the main character in the story?
2. Where does the story take place?
3. Who were the Arawaks?
4. Identify four animals that the Arawaks hunted?
5. Why did the Spanish Priest engrave a map of gold and gave it to the four guardians?
6. Where did Jonathan find the Manatee?
7. Where was the Manatee's section of the map hidden?
8. Where did Jonathan find the Alligator?
9. Where was the Alligator's section of the map found?
10. What did the Iguana eat?
11. Explain how Jonathan captured the Iguana.
12. Where did the Iguana hide his section of the map?
13. How did Jonathan capture the flamingo?
14. Where did Jonathan find the Arawak village?
15. Why did the Arawaks treat Jonathan with great respect?
16. Suggest another title for the story.
17. Create a list of three things that are fact in the story and three things that are fiction in the story.

EXPRESS YOURSELF

Pretend that you were one of the Arawak villagers; explain what happened when Jonathan arrived in the village.

JONATHAN AND THE SEA MONSTER

1. Who is the main character in the story?
2. Why was the Mermaid crying?
3. How did Jonathan get the Mermaid to the Coast?
4. How was Jonathan able to breathe under water?
5. Why is the Great Barrier Reef called the Rainforest of the Ocean?
6. Give another name for a Sea Turtle.
7. Identify one reason why the Sea Turtle wanted to eat the Mermaid?
8. Why did Jonathan let the Stingray go?
9. Why did the shark want to eat the Mermaid?
10. Describe the sea monster?
11. Why did the Mer people come to help fight the sea monster?
12. In your own words, describe how the sea monster was defeated.
13. What did the Mer people give Jonathan for helping the Mermaid?
14. Suggest another title for the story.
15. Create a list of three things that are fact in the story and three things that are fiction in the story.

EXPRESS YOURSELF

Jonathan was a very brave boy. Agree or Disagree. Using information from the story, support your answer.

JONATHAN AND THE FIGHT FOR THE PIRATE'S TREASURE

1. Who is the main character in the story?
2. What did the map show?
3. In what year did Woodes Rogers come to the Bahamas?
4. Why did the pirates drink from the Creek of Youth?
5. Where was the Creek of Youth located?
6. Who did Jonathan go to for information on the pirate's treasure?
7. Identify three pirates who were Captains?
8. Who was Master Shang?
9. Give the names of the three Cays where the pirates could be found?
10. What weapons were used by the first pirate?
11. What was the name of the first pirate?
12. What weapons were used by the second pirate?
13. What was the name of the second pirate?
14. What weapons were used by the third pirate?
15. What was the name of the third pirate?
16. Describe the female pirate?
17. Which pirate wore Rasta braids?
18. Why was Jonathan unable to defeat the third pirate?
19. Where was the treasure located?
20. Suggest another title for the story.
21. Create a list of three things that are factual in the story and three things that are fictional.

EXPRESS YOURSELF

Imagine you are the writer of this story, complete the story by determining what happens after Jonathan remembers Grandpa Roy's words "Once a pirate, always a pirate"

JONATHAN AND THE GREEN MILADER

1. Who is the main character in the story?
2. Why was Jonathan excited?
3. Who was Mr. Toadler?
4. Why did Jonathan enjoy talking with Mr. Toadler?
5. Why was the entire village sad?
6. What did the old women in the village believe had happened to Mr.Toadler?
7. What did Mr. Toadler tell the police?
8. Why did, the nurse and doctor did not believe Mr. Toadler's story?
9. How do you know that Jonathan's mother believed Mr. Toadler's story?
10. What did Jonathan's mother call the creature?
11. Why was Mr. Toadler happy to see Jonathan?
12. List three items Jonathan took with him when he went in search of the creature?
13. Where did the creature live?
14. Explain in your own words how Jonathan captured the creature.
15. What did the creature do with Jonathan after he captured him?
16. Describe the creature's appearance.
17. Where did the creature come from?
18. Explain how Jonathan escaped from the creature?
19. How did Jonathan convince the villagers that the creature was real?
20. Suggest another title for the story?
21. Create a list of three things that are fact in the story and three things that are fiction.

EXPRESS YOURSELF

Imagine you are the Green Milander; describe how you came to live on the island of Andros, how you survived and your encounters with human beings.
Or
Write a Part to the story telling why the villagers could not find the Green Milander

JASMINE AND THE TREE OF LIFE

1. Who is the main character in the story?
2. Why did Jasmine race home from school?
3. How did Columbus describe the unique tree?
4. Which settlement did Jasmine go to first?
5. What did Teta want to teach Jasmine?
6. Identify one thing that Teta taught Jasmine about bush medicine?
7. Name the second settlement where Jasmine stopped.
8. Identify one thing that Dada taught Jasmine about bush medicine?
9. Name the third settlement where Jasmine stopped?
10. Identify one thing that Meme taught Jasmine about bush medicine?
11. How long did Jasmine stay with each of the bush medicine women?
12. When could the Tree of Life be seen?
13. Where was the Tree of Life located?

JONATHAN, GRANDPA ROY AND THE ADELINE

1. Name the two main characters in the story.
2. When was Grandpa Roy born?
3. Who was David in the story?
4. What was the name of Grandpa Roy's Vessel?
5. Why was Grandpa Roy anxious to get to Nassau?
6. Who or what was Mr. High Cay?
7. Why did the ghostly pirate board the vessel?
8. How did Grandpa Roy and Jonathan get rid of the ghostly pirate?
9. Did Grandpa Roy check the seas and the skies?
10. What type of storm did Grandpa Roy and the vessel encounter?
11. According to the story, what does it mean to "spring a leak".
12. What was the huge metallic creature that rose from below the surface?
13. How did the navy men help Grandpa Roy?
14. Suggest another title for the story.
15. Create a list of three things that are factual in the story and three things that are fictional in the story.

EXPRESS YOURSELF

Pretend that you are Grandpa Roy. Retell your adventure to a group of villagers around a camp fire.

JASMINE AND THE TAR BABY

1. Who is the main character in the story?
2. Why did Jonathan let Jasmine win the race?
3. What crops did the children's mother grow in her yard?
4. What animal did Jonathan's mother tell him to go and feed?
5. Why did the villagers use Tar babies?
6. Why did Jasmine want to catch the Tar baby?
7. Where did Jasmine search for the Tar baby?
8. What type of tree did Jasmine climb?
9. Why did Jasmine climb the tree?
10. What happened to the bird that flew too close to the Tar baby?
11. Suggest one reason why Jasmine did not light the Tar baby afire.
12. Why did Jasmine want the Tar Baby to follow her?
13. What happened to Jasmine's clothes while she was running?
14. What happened to Jasmine's shoes?
15. What happened to the Tar baby?
16. How did the villagers react when they realized that Jasmine had destroyed the Tar baby?
17. Suggest another title for the story?
18. Create a list of three things that are factual in the story and three things that are fictional in the story.

EXPRESS YOURSELF

In your own words, retell how Jasmine found and destroyed the Tar baby.

JASMINE AND JONATHAN AND THE SEARCH FOR THE CREEK OF YOUTH

1. Who are the main characters in the story?
2. Where did the two children want their father to take them?
3. Why did the children's father go "chapping"?
4. What proof is there to show that the Children's father was a good fisherman?
5. Why were the fishing grounds called?
6. What was the legend that accompanied "Old House?"
7. Why did the children go to the old crab?
8. What did the children take with them on their adventure?
9. Where did the old crab live?
10. What did the children give the old crab as a gift?
11. What did the children promise the old crab?
12. Describe the vicious creature that lived in the Creek?
13. How did the children kill the creature?
14. Suggest another title for the story?
15. Create a list of three things that are factual in the story and three things that are fictional.

EXPRESS YOURSELF

Pretend that you are either Jasmine or Jonathan; give an eye witness account of how you killed the Creek Creature. You may use any of the vocabulary words to assist you in your story.

JONATHAN AND THE HUNT FOR THE WOOD LAND BEAST

1. Who is the main character in the story?
2. Why did Jonathan and his father enter the contest?
3. What was the prize for winning the contest?
4. What is a wild hog?
5. Where do wild hogs live?
6. Name two things that wild hogs eat?
7. Why was the beast considered a special wild hog?
8. Who was Poke?
9. Why did Jonathan go to his friend the Chickcharnie?
10. Where did the old owl live?
11. Why did the old owl decide to help Jonathan and his father?
12. What did the old owl tell Jonathan and his father?
13. What does BLC mean?
14. Do you think BLC was important to the economy of Andros? Explain your answer.
15. Why did Jonathan and his father run behind the beast for hours? What did the villagers say when Jonathan and his father returned with the beast?
16. Suggest another name for the story?
17. Create a list of three things that are factual in the story and three things that are fictional.

EXPRESS YOURSELF

If you could be any of the characters in the story, which one would you be and why.

JONATHAN AND JASMINE AND THE SECRET OF THE TWO KEYS

1. Name the two main characters in the story?
2. Why was Jasmine singing?
3. Why did Jonathan want Jasmine to stop singing?
4. How did Jonathan get Jasmine to stop singing?
5. What do you think the "L" and the "H" on the two keys stood for?
6. Why did the ghost haunt the building?
7. How did the children get from home to Andros Town?
8. Why did Jasmine carry a camera on the adventure?
9. Why did the children take a cutlass with them?
10. What door did the first key open?
11. What did the children find in the hidden room?
12. Do you think the children understood the importance of the map they found?
13. Why did the children run away and leave everything behind?
14. Suggest another name for the story?
15. Create a list of three things that are factual in the story and three things that are fictional?

EXPRESS YOURSELF

Have you ever visited a strange place like a deserted lighthouse, an old building, a haunted house or a cemetery? Describe your experience.

JASMINE AND JONATHAN AND THE PRICKLE PATCH

1. Who are the main characters in the story?
2. Why were the villagers staying indoors?
3. Where were the prickles coming from?
4. What was bringing the prickles?
5. Why was the children's mother sad?
6. What did the children decide to do?
7. How did the children dress for their adventure?
8. Why were the children unable to eat their lunch?
9. How did the children intend to destroy the prickle patch?
10. How were the children going to use the blue hole?
11. Do you think the children's plan was a good one? Explain your answer.
12. Who joined the children in the blue hole?
13. How did Jonathan Figure out the way home?
14. Suggest another title for the story?
15. Create a list of three things that are factual in the story and three things that are fictional?

EXPRESS YOURSELF

Describe an adventure that you have had before. Include where it took place, what you did, who was with you and how you felt during the adventure.

JONATHAN AND JASMINE AND AN AFTERNOON WITH GRANDPA ROY

Who are the main characters in the story?

What were the children doing when their mother came into the room?

Why did the children's mother scream when she entered the room?

What did the children's mother tell the children to do?

Why did the children go to Grandpa Roy?

What did the children meet Grandpa Roy doing?

What did the children eat as a snack?

What did Grandpa Roy do every morning before going to school?

In which settlement was the school located?

What did Grandpa Roy have breakfast and lunch everyday?

Who teased the Love Hill boys when they got to school?

Name three places where Grandpa Roy worked other than Andros?

Who rescued Grandpa Roy out of the cemetery?

Where did Grandpa Roy and his cousin drop the two ladies whom they give a ride?

Describe how the villagers dressed for the wedding reception.

Why did Lil Thing beat up everybody?

How was Lil Thing subdued?

What was the moral of the story in the Wedding reception?

Suggest another name for the story.

Create a list of three things that are fact in the story and three things that are fiction.

EXPRESS YOURSELF

According to the events in Grandpa Roy's life, what type of person do you think he is?

Or

Summarize in your own words the incident involving Lil Thing.